FREEDRIC'S AIRPLANE

Life is what happens when you're designing your airplane.

Gorg Huff &
Paula Goodlett

Cover art and design by Laura Givens and Joy Joseph
Line editing and Proof reading by Mary Hayward

Gorg Huff & Paula Goodlett
Visit my website at www.WarSpell.com or our Facebook page WarSpell
https://www.facebook.com/groups/1192614074680069

CONTENTS

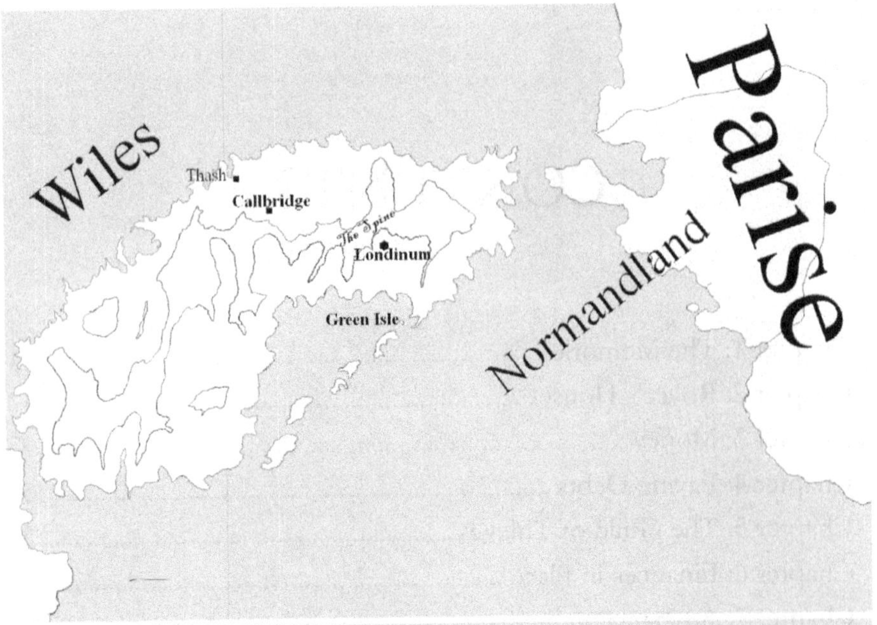
Wiles
Thash
Callbridge
The Spine
Londinum
Green Isle
Normandland
Parise

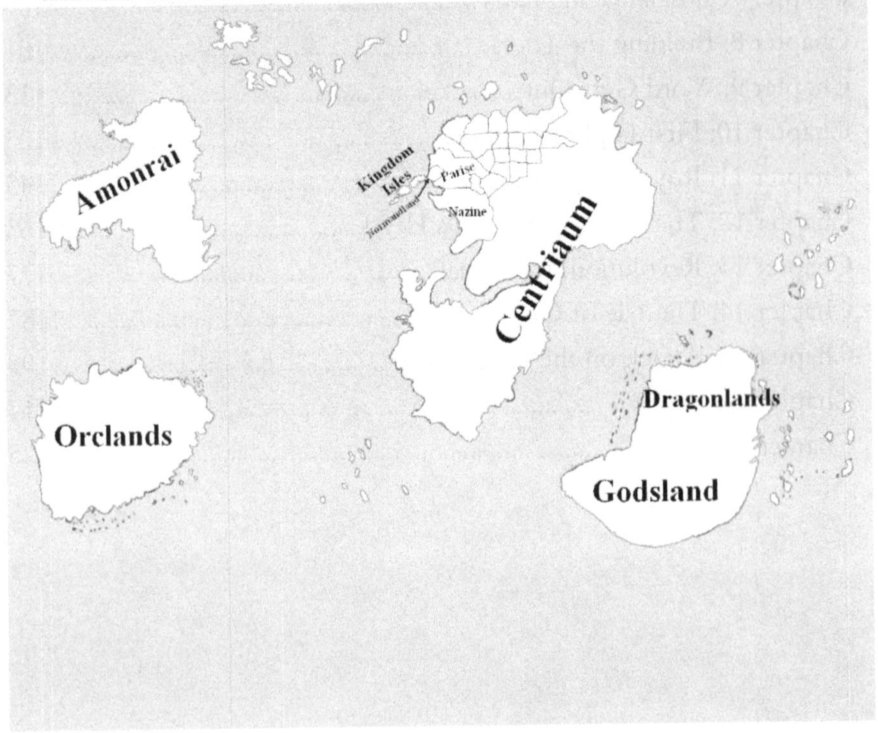
Amonrai
Kingdom Isles
Parise
Nazine
Normandland
Centriaum
Dragonlands
Orclands
Godsland

CHAPTER 1: THE MEMORIES

Location: Conley's Magic Shop, Callbridge
Time: Midafternoon, 5 Pago, 989AF

Freedric the Incompetent dipped his quill in the inkwell and started to write:

The placement of the tines on the comb of cleaning can limit the magical flow so that__

His quill went right through the paper as the image of a metal aircraft wing appeared in his mind. He cursed. He hadn't put a pen through paper since his first year at the wizard academy. Thankfully, this was a report, not a spell. Spells used special paper and ink, both designed to be color accurate in a way that most inks weren't. He carefully put the quill in the holder, then sat back in his chair and examined his new memories.

He remembered his life as Jerry Garman. Jerry Garman, who typed on a computer rather than writing with a pen that had a point made of ivory.

Jerry, who didn't believe in magic, but could design airplanes. And who had played a game called WarSpell many years before. A game in which he played the part of Freedric the Incompetent. A name that he chose for laughs. The nickname from his first year at the wizard academy and bane of Freedric's existence was Jerry Garman's joke. At the same time, Freedric remembered that first year at the wizard academy. All the mistakes he'd made, and the embarrassment they caused him. The real danger that he would be sent down. The effort it had taken to force his mind into the patterns necessary to craft a spell out of nothingness. And the still present habit of meticulous care that he used to compensate for his mind's tendency to wander.

In remembering the game, Freedric remembered the other players and the characters they played. There was Brian Davis who played Sir Brian Royce, an amulet wizard who had funded their first dungeon crawl. Brian had been the Gamemaster as well, which Jerry had felt was cheating, and was one of the reasons that he and Tim Walters had dropped out of the game. Tim, an electrical engineer, was probably the nerdiest nerd in the whole group and they were all nerds. Tim had played Alvin the Bard, a musician and player who Freedric liked quite well, but trusted even less than he trusted Pip. Pip, played by Betty Davis, Brian's wife. "Oh gods!" Freedric muttered, "Pip was a girl." Pip, who had appeared to be a lad of no more than fourteen was actually a woman of twenty-two. Something Alvin had known from the beginning and never shared with any of them. Pip was a thief who was along to open locks. Freedric had never liked Pip or trusted him . . . well, her, he guessed now. And from the game it was apparent that Pip wanted him to dislike her so Freedric wouldn't learn that she was a woman.

Yahg, a half-orc warrior who Freedric found difficult to know, was played by John Kipler, a paraplegic programmer.

If Freedric had the memories of Jerry Garman, did Brian Royce have the memories of Brian Davis? Did Pip have the memories of Betty, Alvin remember Tim, and did Yahg remember John?

It would probably be a good idea to find out.

Carefully, because Freedric did just about everything carefully, Freedric cleaned and put away his tools and set about leaving the shop where he worked. He was a small, spare man with a bent nose and black hair and eyes.

His boss stopped him. "Where are you going?"

"I have some errands to run."

"I don't pay you to run errands. Get back to your desk if you don't want to lose your job."

Freedric was still Freedric, but he now had the memories of Jerry Garman and those memories did two things for him. First, they let him see how much the business needed him, and second, with Jerry's knowledge of aeronautics, he realized that he didn't need this job. Jerry could make an airplane.

"Fire me if you want, but I have errands to run. I'll be back tomorrow to pick up my final pay, if you decide to fire me. Or, if I still have a job here, to finish that report on why your magic combs aren't working as they should."

Then he walked out, feeling both terrified and exhilarated.

The last Freedric had heard, Alvin was playing at a tavern on Tanners Street. If he remembered right from the last game they'd played, Alvin was a fifth-level bard. In Freedric's day to day world they didn't have levels. It was just that magic users like everyone else got better with practice. But in the game, there were levels and rules about how many spells a character of a given level might craft or cast. There were also categories, types of magic users. Bard was a subcategory of Natural Wizard. Like all natural wizards, they internalize spells rather than crafting them like a book wizard. Bards could use their music to amplify or change their magic. It also made spells of persuasion and illusion easier than spells that actually did stuff. All this was running through Freedric's mind as he walked down the street. He turned on Riverside and started walking downriver and a few minutes later out of Callbridge proper. Tanneries and other smelly occupations were by law placed downriver.

Location: Glenda's Tavern, Tanners Street, Callbridge
Time: Midafternoon, 5 Pago, 989AF

Alvin the Bard was barely getting by. That bastard Brian Royce had badmouthed him all over town and nearly gotten him burned as a witch. So he wasn't allowed to play in taverns in Callbridge proper and he had to be very careful about the magic he used. He tuned his lute and looked at the crowd. It would be so easy to weave a friendship spell into his song to encourage the patrons of this dive to be a bit more generous.

He looked over at the tavern owner and reconsidered. Glenda was watching him like a hawk. She had almost no magic, but she did have the sight, and the deal was: he could play, but if he used magic, he was out.

He strummed a cord and all of a sudden he had the song "Blowing in the Wind" playing in his head. He stopped playing when he saw Glenda coming over. The stage was a single step up from the earthen floor of the tavern.

Glenda got to the stage and grabbed his arm. "What did you do?"

"Wasn't me, Glenda. I swear. It was done to me."

"What was done to you then?" Glenda asked. She was about as far as you could get from the image of Glenda the Good from the *Wizard of Oz*. She was on the far side of forty and overweight, dressed in a homespun undyed and poorly sewn tube dress that had the stains of preparing today's meals on it. Yet Glenda *was* good. A woman kind enough to give even a ne'er-do-well like Alvin a second, or was it third, chance. He didn't want to blow that.

"I'm not sure. I have the memories of someone else. He knows songs, but was no bard. He had no magic of any sort but he knew things. And now I know them. Glenda, I remember *being* him. Living his life, his whole life . . ." He wouldn't ask Glenda to believe this next part. He didn't believe it and he remembered it. Years ago, Tim Walters had played a game of WarSpell. A game of improvisational acting that used dice. In that game, Tim Walters had played a pretense called Alvin the Bard.

Glenda shook his arm. "Prove it then, play a song that the other fellow knew. Mind, no magic." She stepped back from the stage but not far.

Alvin sang. He sang "Blowing in the Wind" because that was what Tim Walters had been listening to when whatever happened happened.

And he tried not to infuse the song with magic. He really did. But the song had a magic all its own and it would not be stilled. He changed "cannon balls fly" to "catapult launch" because this world had no cannon. But other than that, he left the lyrics as they were. He'd been listening to the Peter, Paul & Mary cover of the song and soon enough his lute was accompanied by a guitar and his voice was accompanied by gentle harmonies.

The song finished and released him from the spell, and he looked up to see a silent tavern. Every face was turned toward him and there was not a dry eye in the house. He looked over at Glenda, and she too was staring with wet eyes. Then her face hardened.

"I'm sorry, Glenda. I wasn't trying to," Alvin pleaded. "It was the song. It would have its way, no matter my wishes."

"Come down from the stage, Alvin," she commanded. "I don't doubt you, Alvin, but don't you see? That makes it worse. I can't have uncontrolled magic in my place. Can't."

Alvin argued, he pleaded, he *didn't* use magic, Glenda would see that. A half an hour or so later he was out of the tavern with a few copper pence for his parting. He was looking around when he saw Freedric the Incompetent approaching. Freedric who'd been played by Jerry Garman. And that was when it occurred to Alvin that if he had Tim's memories, Freedric might have Jerry's

It was a better option than any other he had. "Jerry?" he asked as he walked toward Freedric. "Do you recall Jerry Garman?"

"I do," Freedric agreed. "I take it you remember being Tim Walters?"

"I do," Alvin agreed in turn. "If you and I have the memories of our players, what about the rest?"

"It's possible, but I, or rather Jerry, only played WarSpell for that one campaign. The only WarSpell character Jerry ever played was me."

"Same with Tim. But I know from Tim's memories that Betty played several and John Kipler was a regular. The question is does that mean they have the memories of all the players they played?"

"I wouldn't even speculate," Freedric said. "But that's the reason I'm here. You were the only one aside from Brian Royce that I had any idea where to find and even if he does have Brian Davis' memories, I'm still not sure I trust him."

"Right," Alvin said. "Brian, being both player character and gamemaster didn't bother Tim as much as it did Jerry. He just found the game less fun than he hoped."

"It's not that," Freedric said. "At least not mostly. I, by which I mean Freedric, not Jerry, was always a bit creeped out by Bryan Royce."

Alvin nodded agreement. He'd had the same feeling about Royce all the time he'd known the man. And from some of the things Brian Davis had said when not in character, it was probably justified.

"I was wondering if you would know how to contact Pip and Yahg?" Freedric asked him.

"No and yes," Alvin said. "I don't know where either of them is, but there's a bardic spell that lets you sing a message to someone you know, and get a return message if the circumstances are right. They need to be somewhere quiet and at rest, but not asleep. Now would probably be a pretty good time, but I need to be in a quiet safe place to cast the spell, and I don't have one at the moment."

"Your rooms?"

"I don't have a room. I was hoping to earn enough for a cot in one of the doss houses down here, but getting Tim's memories messed that up good and proper."

"I have a room. It's not much, just a single room, with a desk and a cot."

"Luxury," Alvin assured him.

"Then follow me. I wonder how Pip and Yahg are doing?"

Location: Dwarven Tunnels, near Callbridge
Time: Midafternoon, 5 Pago, 989AF

Pip wondered how she'd let herself be talked into this. Alvin could talk birds down out of trees, but Brian Royce . . . All he had was money. Just at the moment she needed money. Her dues to the thieves' guild were in arrears and if they didn't get their money, she was going to get hurt.

Dwarven tunnels were dangerous. They had been created by the dwarves at the height of the Empire of Rime and abandoned for hundreds of years. In the case of the tunnels in the Kingdom Isles, they'd been abandoned since before the fall of Rime.

The Dwarven Empire had used a lot of magic. That magic was left unattended after the dwarves had been forced out. It had festered under ground, changing things.

Brian had an amulet of light on the top of his staff. It cast a decent light about as bright as a lamp. Most of the magic lights in this section of the tunnels had either gone out centuries ago or had converted over time to project strange illusions.

For this, none of that mattered. Picking a lock was best done by feel, so she closed her eyes. Carefully, she worked the lockpick, moving it around in the lock, feeling the tumblers one by one. There were four and then a click. And in the instant, Pip knew she was dead. The door blew out. There was a fireball spell on it.

She was down on the stone floor with her body shattered and bleeding out. *I don't want to die*, she prayed with no notion of who she was praying to.

* * *

Each Merge is unique. Which character is chosen, of all the characters a player has played, is affected by any number of factors. In this case, it was because the character desperately wanted help.

She got it. Every wound, even every scar she'd ever received, was healed instantly and she got the memories of Betty Cartwright. Who'd been Betty Davis when she'd been playing this game, but took back her maiden name after the divorce. She remembered Brian Davis, telling her after the game that she'd had a rod of fireball in the pack of stuff she'd lifted. Knowing what was coming from her memories of the game, she started looking for the rod of fireball.

Out of the blown door came a pack of cave cougars. They were black with large eyes and they screamed at the light that Brian was carrying and went for him first. Brian swung the staff with the light on its tip.

Yahg went for the cats. Yahg was a half-orc, and built like one. He pulled one of the cats off Brian and threw it into the far wall, then another had him by the arm and Yahg went down to one knee. He was still fighting, but he was losing.

By then two of the cats were looking her way. Pip pulled the rod of fireball and pointed it. She was a fifth level thief and could usually guess how to activate a magical item.

She activated this one just fine.

A fireball bloomed, Yahg, Brian and all the cave cougars were in the blast. The cats were thrown against the walls of the dwarven hall. So were Yahg and Brian Royce. All six of the cave cougars were broken, smoldering messes.

It wasn't the willful murder of her companions. She'd just been terrified and hadn't known what else to do. Then Yahg stood up.

"Uh, hi, Yahg," she said, half hiding the rod of fireball behind her. She noted in passing that his armor was smoking and he was patting it out. But his bright green hair wasn't even singed.

Yahg looked around, then back at Pip, and grinned. "So you're a girl."

Now Pip was nervous in an entirely different way. Did the explosion rip open her shirt? She looked down. It had, but her breasts weren't exposed. Then she realized that since she had Betty's memories maybe Yahg had John's. "John?"

"Yes," Then looking down at the light green down on the back of his hand. "No. I'm still Yahg, but I have his memories and, I'm guessing, his intelligence." He looked around. "But not his squeamishness, I don't think," Yahg said as he stepped over and started examining what was left of Brian Royce, patting out the burning bits as he went.

"Come over here," he said. "You're a criminal and if I remember right you have the identify magical items skill." He wasn't referring to her membership in the thieves' guild. He was talking about her character class in the game WarSpell and the identify magical item was a class skill that thieves could choose from a list of available skills. Those were Betty's memories, but they were *all* hers now.

Carefully, Pip got up and moved to the corpse of Brian Royce. She remembered her husband, Brian Davis, who'd run the game and played Brian Royce. And in that campaign he'd been the only one whose character survived. Her character and John's had died. Brian had rolled his save behind the game master's screen and Betty was pretty sure he'd been cheating and justifying it, as a way to keep the game running. Brian had always been good at justifying his cheating.

Both Betty and John had had to roll up new characters. She wondered if Bridget, the natural wizard, had gotten Betty's memories too. "Yahg, do you think Simon the acrobat got John's memories too?" Simon the acrobat was the character that John had rolled up for this campaign after Yahg was killed, just like Bridget was the character Betty had rolled up after Pip was killed.

"Interesting thought," Yahg said in his deep voice, but speaking in John's style and diction, with even a little of John's Texas drawl. "We should look them up, him and Bridget, to find out. Freedric and Alvin, as well. But later!

"For now, I need you to find the key to Royce's vault. Knowing Brian Royce, and Brian Davis, I figure he had it on him. If I'm right, it will probably be magical."

* * *

Pip didn't throw up examining Royce, but it was a near thing. He'd been thrown across the passage and his skull was shattered, probably when he hit the wall of the corridor. Had she killed him?"

"Do you think I killed him with the rod of fireballs?"

"Yes. Me too," Yahg said.

Pip looked up nervously and Yahg laughed. "It was your best option given the circumstances. What worries me is he didn't come back. In the game we both died, but not by fireball and Brian survived. This time I died by fireball and so did Brian. I was healed and so were you. That first fireball that went off when you picked the lock was fatal.

"Pip, no, Betty, where were you living, on Earth I mean, just before this happened?"

"New York. I was working as a bank teller. I went to bed around ten thirty just like every night. That's the last thing I remember as Betty."

"I was in L.A. doing web design. I was awake. It was happening all over the world. It started on the east coast, so it probably hit you in your sleep. But there was news about it all over the web. That's right. Just before I was here, I saw a news report. A reporter, a woman, had gotten the memories of this elf that she played. I bet it went both ways."

He waved a hand in a gesture that was a strange mix of Yahg and John. "Never mind for now. You keep looking for Royce's keys. I'm going to check out that room." He left.

Almost automatically, she started to pocket the most valuable of Brian Royce's goods. Then she stopped. Along with Betty's memories, she'd gotten Betty's morals. So she laid out everything,

Five minutes later he was back. "Some armor and an ax," he reported, "and a bunch of bones. Mostly animals. What about you?"

Pip pointed. "The key was in the staff. You remove the amber stone and the bronze dragon claw is the key."

"I guess Betty's having an influence."

"I guess," Pip agreed. "I don't know how long it's going to last. But for now at least, I don't steal from my friends."

Yahg nodded seriously. "Okay let's get Royce into that room over there and we'll need to strip him entirely. Then pile the cave cougars on top. We want as much time as we can get before the body is found."

"Why?" Pip asked, then she knew from Betty's memories. Brian Royce was a remittance man. When it became known that he was dead, two things would happen. The remittance would stop being sent to the counting house, and his relatives would send someone to take possession of everything he owned. So Pip nodded and helped Yahg hide the body.

As they worked, she got the feeling that Alvin the Bard wanted to tell her something or maybe ask her something. But she was busy and didn't really hear the message.

CHAPTER 2: ROYCE'S HOUSE

Location: Freedric's Room, Callbridge
Time: Evening, 5 Pago, 989AF

"It's no go," Alvin said. "I've been trying to reach Pip and Yahg for the last hour and nothing."

"What about, Royce?"

"I don't really want to talk to Royce," Alvin said with a bitterness that surprised Freedric.

Then it made sense. After they quit Royce, he'd blackened Freedric's name mostly by saying that "incompetent" was an apt descriptor. It had made getting work as a book wizard difficult. That had led Freedric to the job at the magical device shop, where everyone was incompetent. "He badmouthed you?"

"All over town. Insisting that I was casting spells on people to get their money."

Freedric didn't actually disbelieve the slur. It seemed the sort of thing that Alvin might well do, especially if money was tight. It wasn't the sort of thing that Tim Walters, electrical engineer, would do. So Freedric lifted an eyebrow and asked, "Was there any truth to the accusations?"

Alvin started to bluster, then just shook his head. "A little, not much. It can happen by accident when the music takes you."

Freedric nodded. "I got some sausage rolls from a vendor on the corner. Eat and try again a little later."

Like most rooms, Freedric's didn't have cooking facilities. He knew some spells that would heat a meal, but mostly it was simpler to just buy a sausage roll from a street vender. While they ate sausage rolls and drank vegetable broth, they talked about Freedric's idea of building an airplane.

"There are flying spells, you know."

"Yes, there are. But I don't know any of them. Do you?"

"Just Lift." The Lift spell was a fourth level spell that allowed whatever it was cast on to float in the air like a balloon. The thing it was cast on had to be willing or inanimate. It couldn't be used on an unwilling being.

"How much can you levitate and for how long?"

"A few hundred pounds," Alvin said. "I don't know for sure. I've only levitated myself and my gear." He pointed at the cloth case that held his lute.

They finished their meal and Freedric asked Alvin about electric motors. Which brought to Alvin's mind synthesizers and they talked size, resistance, and the making of batteries, while Freedric took notes.

Then Freedric went to work on the designs for a small airplane, while Alvin tried again to contact Pip or Yahg.

Location: Royce Townhouse, Callbridge
Time: Evening, 5 Pago, 989AF

"You sure this is a good idea?" Pip asked. "What if Royce's servants wake up and call the city guard?

"Pretty sure they won't wake up," Yahg said, without turning his eyes away from the alley, "and even surer that they won't call the guard. Get to it. I'll keep watch for passersby."

Muttering, Pip got to it. She picked the lock to the tradesman's entrance of Brian Royce's townhouse. The lock clicked, Pip opened the door, and they slipped in.

Yahg closed and locked the door. They looked around.

It was a nice place, clean and well kept. They'd both been here before, but they'd been limited to the tradesman's entrance and the back hall. Which was where they were now, but they were inside, out of sight of neighbors, and there was time. So they proceeded with caution, willing to take all night to be sure. Pip checked carefully for traps while Yahg watched for attacks.

Royce hadn't been a trusting sort. Yahg was pretty sure there were no living servants, just magical ones. However, Royce had had a variety of magical ones. He'd had appearances to maintain. That meant the appearance of servants. Along with the standard servant spell, Royce had used *Sims*.

A *Sim* was a sort of magical servant that was based heavily on a person or animal. It was a 14th level spell and it was a ceremony spell. For a wizard to perform the ceremony took a full day, during which the person or animal being copied had to remain in one container and the materials for the copy had to be in the other. Both containers were magic items. They had to be made, then have the spell cast into them, and finally aged for the better part of ten years. That was what was needed to produce the equipment that the spell was cast through. The wizard moved between the two containers, so a wizard couldn't cast the spell on themselves. And it wouldn't do a lot of good anyway, because though they could invoke magical items, the copies couldn't craft or cast spells. It could be performed on an unwilling person, but the person had to be kept in the first container.

And if the person wasn't willing, that usually involved chains. If the person being copied was unwilling, they got a Mental Toughness roll to make the spell go wrong. The spell going wrong usually meant that the *Sim* was created, but was hostile rather than loyal to the wizard crafting the spell.

On the upside, the *Sim* was a close to perfect copy of the person or animal copied and would last potentially forever. It didn't eat, but it did need to rest, and recharge, twelve hours out of twenty-four, in an especially made container. The charging containers were also magical items, but they weren't nearly as expensive.

Sims didn't age, but could be damaged or destroyed. Royce had a maid and a butler that were *Sims* and half a dozen permanent servant spells.

Yahg knew about the *Sim* spell because John Kipler had played WarSpell a lot, and been in parties with wizards who had cast it. Though John usually played a warrior of some sort, he'd read up on the game and was familiar with wizard spells of all sorts. This was one of those that fell somewhere between a book wizard and an amulet wizard.

The only reason that Yahg knew about the *Sims* was that Royce talked about stuff in front of Yahg that he was confident Yahg wouldn't understand. John had used his lowest stat for Yahg's intelligence, an 82. So Royce had been right. It was only after Yahg got John's memories and intelligence that he realized what Royce's comments meant.

Finally Pip got the door from the back hall to the main house unlocked and they went in.

One of the servant spells, a ghostly apparition of a liveried footman offered to take the "master's cloak." Yahg looked at Pip with a lifted eyebrow.

Pip looked at the staff in her hand and said. "I guess it does more than I thought, but don't expect it to work when his maid and butler wake up."

"I don't think they will," Yahg said again. "I think they're *Sims*.

"*Sims?*" Pip asked, then. "Oh! Damn it, Yahg. You could have told me that an hour ago."

Yahg shrugged green furred shoulders. "I wasn't sure. I'm still not. Even if they are *Sims*, we're going to have to figure out how to wake them and how to get them on our side.

"I may have a thought on that," Pip said, looking at Royce's staff which she still carried. Then she looked around the room.

The room was lit with amber light globes enchanted to operate continuously. There were little covers that were placed over them if you didn't want light.

Yahg carefully sat on a settee in the front hall and said, "I'm going to sit right here and relax while you search the place. My skills don't run to detecting traps and my guess is that Royce left a few."

Pip nodded and started examining the doors, bookcases and windows carefully.

Yahg waited and used a technique he had from John Kipler's memories to relax and consider calmly. John had used it both to help him think calmly about programs he was working on and to keep calm and relaxed while the doctors worked on his increasingly failing body.

It was in this state that he got Alvin's message. "*Do you remember John Kipler? Who Played Freedric?*"

He thought back, "*Freedric was played by Jerry Garman. Come to Royce's townhouse.*" He opened his eyes. Pip was carefully examining a door. "Pip, step away for a moment."

Pip stepped back from the door. "What is it?"

"I just heard from Alvin. He asked if I remembered John Kipler and who played Freedric. I told him to come here."

"Why'd you tell him that?"

"Because if he knows about John Kipler, he has Tim Walters memories."

"And?"

"And if he has Tim Walter's memories, we want him on our side. After all, he kept the secret of your gender for as long as he and Jerry were in the game. I didn't know you were female until I got John Kipler's memories."

"That wasn't all that long, only a few weeks while they were with us, and two weeks since they dropped out of the game. That's two weeks, our time. Betty was fifty-two when I got her memories." Pip considered. "Okay he knew and kept quiet, but that was Alvin. Tim always struck me as a little creepy."

Yahg laughed. "He was, but no more than most guys. Including me. He just didn't know how to go about it. John didn't either, but Yahg does."

"And you do?"

"Yahg does. John Kipler probably understood the fair sex even less than Tim. The point is, we need him on our side or we need to be rid of him."

"Rid of him?"

"Yes. That's what I mean. We need him on our side or dead. We don't want anyone who could out us as 'being possessed,' or do you want to end up burned at the stake?"

Pip looked at Yahg in something close to shock, which wasn't what he expected from Pip. "Remember, Pip, we're living in a much tougher time than Betty and John did. Don't let Betty's sensibilities blind you to how the world works."

* * *

Twenty minutes later there was a knock at the front door.

When Yahg opened it, not only Alvin but Freedric the Incompetent were standing on the front steps.

"Come in." Yahg stepped back and they came in. He shut the door behind them. The servant came and took their coats.

Freedric was looking around. "I see Pip, but where's Royce?"

"He didn't make it," Pip said.

"You went back to the Dwarven tunnels?" Alvin asked.

"We did," Pip said.

Freedric nodded, then made a gesture and said a quick phrase in something that sounded like Latin. "I just cast see magic." He looked around the room. "There are concentrations of magic there." He pointed. "And there and there."

It hadn't taken Freedric more than a moment to figure out what was going on. With Royce dead, Yahg and Pip were planning to loot his townhouse for anything they could find. That left the question of why Yahg had invited Freedric and Alvin to the party. He looked over at Alvin.

Alvin also saw magic fields, but not as well as a wizard who'd cast see magic. On the other hand, since those fields were a standard part of his world, he had an advantage in spotting spells that were "unfriendly."

Alvin said, "I'll help Pip," then joined her in her search for traps and secret panels and passages.

* * *

An hour later, they had finished a cursory examination and defused the traps that Royce placed as he left home. That was made much easier by their possession of Royce's "keys," which were part of his staff. They had found two hidden panels in the back wall under the staircase of the front hall. The front hall of Royce's townhouse was less corridor than room. It was twenty feet wide with a staircase leading to the second floor, another leading to the basement, a door into the dining room, and another into the back hall and the storage rooms.

The townhouse was now treating them as guests, as long as they stayed away from Royce's vault, private library and workshop, both of which were on the second floor. Royce had been a fairly adept manufacturer of magical items. They went into the dining room and Freedric instructed one of the servants to cook them dinner.

* * *

Dinner was served a few minutes later. They sat down, ate and talked. Alvin and Freedric found Yahg and Pip to be harder than they'd realized while they were adventuring with them.

It made sense, especially in Freedric's case. His family had been well off enough to pay his way through the wizards college here in Callbridge. But Alvin had probably also had it easier than Yahg and Pip for most of his life. He'd demonstrated a talent for music early, so he'd had opportunities of his own. At least until Brian Royce sullied Alvin's name in his pique over their leaving the exploring group.

On the other hand, Yahg was a half orc fighter in a world where orcs were considered subhuman brutes. Pip was brought up as a thief in a world where a thief could lose their hand or their life if they were caught. They would have found this world a much harsher place than Freedric and Alvin.

Freedric and Alvin, with the memories of Jerry and Tim, had the knowledge of the civil rights movement to inform their understanding, but that didn't make them comfortable with Yahg's easy brutality.

Even Pip was seen to wince.

"If we can wake and control the *Sims*," Yahg said, "we could live here for months, long enough to set up safe residences of our own." Yahg used a knife to spear a slice of roast mutton and put it in his mouth.

"There is the question of the *Sims*," Freedric said. "They are copies of people. Do they have souls, rights? Is it right to?"

"No!" Yahg interrupted, mouth still half full of mutton. He swallowed, shook his head. "No, Freedric, Brian was clear on that. They were automatons, very complex automatons, but not alive. Not even really programmed. All their instructions are ROM. Devices, not people. It's the difference between an expert system and true AI. These are expert systems. Which doesn't mean that they can't *seem* alive. That's what they are designed to do, after all. Mimic a real person."

Freedric didn't think he was lying, but he also didn't think it would matter to Yahg, even this new Yahg, if they were people. A change of subject was needed. "I want to build an airplane."

"What on earth for?" Yahg asked.

"What do you mean? So we can fly."

"You're a book wizard. Cast fly." Pip said.

"One, I don't have fly. Two, I'm not skilled enough to craft it even if the spell was in my spell book, and even if I could and did, fly doesn't move you much faster than a walking horse. An airplane, even a small plane with room for the pilot and three passengers, will take four people—" He pointed at himself, "One," then at Alvin, "two," at Pip, "three," and at Yahg, "four—at a speed of over fifty miles an hour. That's two days travel in an hour."

Yahg was giving Freedric a measuring look and he was reminded that the big half-orc warrior now possessed the memories and intelligence of John Kipler, who made his living as a programer and system designer. "That's the sort of thing that could attract a lot of attention."

"Yes, of course. It could make us all famous," Freedric agreed enthusiastically.

"We're in this house *illegally*," Yahg said. "Famous is something we don't need."

"What we *need*!" Alvin said, "is to not be living *illegally*, anywhere." "Think, John. Yahg had no choice. Before he got John's memories, he had darn few options, and virtually no legal ones. But now you have Yahg's health, strength and skill, but also John Kipler's knowledge and intelligence. Freedric has Jerry's aeronautical engineering knowledge to add to his magic, Pip has Betty's knowledge and abilities to go with her own and I have Tim Walters knowledge of electronics. That's a lot of knowledge, a lot of skills. Put them together right and we can all go legit. Then fame becomes a benefit, not a curse."

"What *I* need is a lot of money," Pip insisted. "That's the only reason I went on that last dungeon crawl with Royce. That and the fact that Betty was married to Brian Davis at the time. Royce promised me enough money to clear my debt to the thieves guild."

Freedric didn't know how the thieves guild worked, but Alvin did. "How much do you owe?"

"Fifteen gold," Pip said.

"That's a bloody fortune." A gold piece was worth what a pound sterling had been worth in the 14th century. Fifteen gold was "Over a year's wage for a skilled craftsman."

"You think I don't know that?"

"How did you manage to get that far in debt?"

"A job went wrong and a guild member got himself killed. I got the blame." She shrugged and added, "If I wanted to buy myself out of the guild, it would take more." She considered her two sets of memories. Pip's life had been a Dickens' novel, only worse. Betty's life hadn't gone great either. After her divorce from Brian, she had two kids to support on her own. Brian had paid child support, but it was rarely on-time and even more rarely the amount needed. She'd worked long hours, but at generally poorly paying jobs until she'd gotten on at the bank. It was still not great pay, but it was a decent job that didn't involve flipping burgers. Betty had most of the way to a degree in accounting and a lot of experience at a bank. She knew how twenty-first century banks worked, but there were no banks in the Kingdom Isles. There were money lenders, who loaned money to nobles, but none of them would even consider hiring Pip.

Betty also read a lot, but that was for entertainment. Pip didn't think Betty knew much of anything useful.

While she'd been thinking about that, the conversation had moved on.

"Do you know how to make black powder?" Yahg asked Alvin.

"Saltpeter, sulfur and charcoal," Pip said. "Grind to fine powder separately. Mix and add water till you have a paste, knead and roll out into a sheet then let dry. Break into fine chunks and you have black powder.

"In what proportion?" Yahg asked.

"Fifteen, three and two," Pip said.

"How did you know that?" Freedric asked.

Alvin laughed. "Because she *reads*, my friends. Betty was always reading. Anytime she wasn't using her hands for something else, she had a book or an e-reader in them." He looked around the dining room. It had a table for eight. There was a door to the kitchen and another to the front hall. One wall had an armoire with plates and flatware. The other had a bookshelf. This was a world without Gutenberg, at least so far, so books were handmade and incredibly expensive. To demonstrate his wealth and education, Brian had this set of twelve books. They were bound in leather and locked in a glass fronted case. "Pip, can you get into that without setting off any traps?"

"Yes, I guess, why?"

"Why, to give you something to read."

"I can't read—" Pip stopped. She had never learned to read, few people did in this world, but Betty . . . Betty could read and do math in her head. She got up and went to the case that held the books, a shrunken head, a glass elephant. A griffin carved from a chunk of amber and half a dozen other knicknacks of uncertain value. She started working, and in a couple of minutes had the case open.

Alvin reached past her and picked up a book, glanced at the gilded letters across the front, and grinned. "A History of the Kingdom Isles." He passed the book to her. "Read a bit of that."

Pip opened the book past the fly leaf and started reading. She could read! It wasn't hard. The language was modern 21st century English. Not even *thys* and *thous.* Pip started to grin. This was a book. A hand copied book. Worth two silvers easy. Not that she could get that for it. The fence that the thieves' guild used would probably only give her five coppers. She turned, holding the book. "Freedric, could you sell this?"

Freedric looked confused. "I guess. Why?"

"Because if I try to sell it, they'll call the city guard and torture me until I tell them where I stole it."

"They'll probably ask me where I got it too," Freedric said. "Without the torture, at least at first."

"Tell them you got it from Brian," Yahg said, "In payment of money owed for services rendered."

"Better yet," Alvin corrected. "Don't tell them who you got it from, just that you received it in payment for spells cast."

Pip turned back to the bookcase. There were eleven more books. Plus the other things.

Freedric looked at the book. It was one that he'd copied for Royce in exchange for money to buy inks for his spell book. He'd copied it by using Z-rocks. A spell loaded into a magical item. Which belonged to Royce. It took Freedric about ten minutes to load, then it would make a copy of the page. That had all happened while Jerry was rolling up the character Freedric before they'd even started playing.

The spell, loaded into the magical item, is considerably faster than a scribe, but it requires an expensive magical item and a wizard to load it. At least a competent amulet wizard. Royce could have done it. He just didn't want to go to the trouble. Six pages an hour, three pages if you copied on both sides, which he had. Ten hours a day is thirty pages a day. This book had taken him over a week.

A week's work from a professional wizard was worth the two silvers Pip said the book was worth, even if you didn't include the cost of the paper and the ink.

Pip was a thief, she could identify and invoke magical items, could she load them? Unlike crafting a full spell, loading a magical item didn't—

Wait a second. What about a printing press? For the moment, the notion of teaching Pip to load magical items completely slipped Freedric's mind.

"Why don't we build a printing press?" He looked around at them.

"Maybe," Yahg said, "but it would be a major project and Gutenberg lost his shirt." He shook his head. "Airplanes, printing presses, black powder for mining and war. Who knows what else? But I'm still a half-orc, Pip's still a thief, and Alvin's still a player.

"You might be able to do that sort of thing, Freedric. You're a licensed book wizard. But the rest of us? We won't be accepted, no matter what we bring. That's just the way the world works."

"So we use Freedric as our front," Alvin said.

"And when he has the profits and the fame? What happens to us?" Pip asked.

"Do you really think I would do that?" Freedric asked. "From what you know of Freedric, and Jerry Garman for that matter. Do you think I would use you and dump you?"

"People change, Freedric," Pip said, "And one of the things that changes them fastest is getting money."

"We aren't going to settle this tonight," Alvin said. "Let's sleep on it.

"Good idea," Freedric agreed. "I have to go to work tomorrow and see if I still have a job."

CHAPTER 3: MONEY

Location: Conley's Magic Shop, Callbridge
Time: Morning, 6 Pago, 989AF (Merge +1)

Freedric entered Conley's Magic Shop to find George Conley waiting. George owned the shop and was a man of business, not a wizard of any sort. He hired crafters to make magical items. He hired amulet loaders to load the magical items. He then stored the magical items away for months or years, until they became stable and easily recharged. Then he sold them. It was a good, solid business that made good money for a man who was already starting out with quite a lot of money. Rather like a Napa Valley Winery, Freedric imagined, based on Jerry's memories of that other world.

Conley was trying to improve the magical items and make them work better with the spells. He was also trying to arrange things so that the magical items would age to usability faster. That was Freedric's job, to examine how the item impacted the spell that was loaded into it, because it was common knowledge that the better the fit, the sooner the magic would stabilize in the item.

"Did you get your business taken care of, Freedric?" Master Conley asked, clearly not happy.

"A good start on it anyway," Freedric replied. At this point, with visions of airplanes dancing in his head, Freedric wasn't at all sure that he wanted to keep this job, whatever Yahg said about keeping a low profile and not changing his routines.

"Just exactly what was that business?" Conley asked, clearly not happy with Freedric's answer.

Freedric looked at him and considered. "A friend of mine, Alvin the Bard, was in a spot of bother and he called me asking for help."

"And just how did he call you? With you sitting at your desk."

"That really isn't your business, Master Conley. And it's not mine to tell. I don't know that it's a secret, but it might be."

Conley's face was getting a little red.

"I'll tell you what, sir. I'll ask Alvin and if he gives me permission, then I'll tell you." Freedric waited a beat, then added, "If I'm still employed here, that is."

"Just what was it that you were thinking about the tines?" George Conley asked.

Freedric suddenly remembered what he'd been doing when he'd gotten Jerry Garman's memories. The tines on the comb of cleaning were interfering with the flow of the magic and not in a good way. What you wanted right there was something approaching laminar flow, not that Freedric had ever heard of laminar flow before yesterday. He smiled as he realized that Jerry's memories were making a lot of things about magical flow clear, as Freedric saw them from a different angle. "You need to remove . . . no, shorten, the tines on the comb. Hm. What you'll want to do is make several combs with different size tines. Have each loaded with the spell of cleaning and see which one works best. I could draw you some designs for your crafters."

"I trust that yesterday's . . . occurrence will be a one time event."

Wait a second, Freedric thought. *For them to know that, they had to have gone through my notes.* His notes, with his spell work and other things that were none of their business. There was nothing about airplanes, of course, or about the magic in Royce's house or printing presses or any of the rest of it. But his memories of the dungeon crawl in search of the dwarf lord's magical items. Notes on Alvin, Bryan Royce, Pip and Yahg. They would have seen those. After he realized that, he was even less anxious to work here.

"No, probably not," Freedric said. "I put Alvin up in my place last night, but I suspect there is more trouble coming." Neither Freedric nor Jerry were particularly good at lying, but he *had* put Alvin up in his place last night. They just hadn't stayed there all night.

Freedric looked around the room. It was full of crafters, most of whom were listening to the discussion, not crafting things.

George Conley followed his glance and his face tightened even more. "Get those drawings done then come see me in my office."

Freedric got the drawings done, then got fired as soon as he'd turned them in. George Conley also shorted him on his pay, insisting that it was a penalty for running off yesterday.

Location: Royce Townhouse, Callbridge
Time: Morning, 6 Pago, 989AF (Merge +1)

Pip carefully removed the amber light jewel from the top of the staff, then she removed the dragon's claw made of jet that it had been placed in. It wasn't complicated, but she was being careful. Magic was dangerous. She placed the dragon's claw into the three depressions in the casket-like box and turned.

The front opened and there was Royce's butler. He opened his eyes. He looked at Pip, then at Yahg and Alvin, back at Pip and said to her, "You're not Brian, but you hold the key. How may I serve you?"

"Who are you?" Yahg asked.

"I am a copy of Brian's younger brother, Charles."

"And the maid?" Yahg asked.

"A copy of our sister, Debra. Our father named us in alphabetical order."

"So you have an older brother?"

"Albert, yes."

"Charles, tell us what happened and how you and Brian ended up here," Pip asked before Yahg could ask another specific question.

"When our father died, Albert inherited, but there was a codicil in the will. The codicil provided Brian, Charles, and Debra with life incomes of eight gold a year each. It was enough to live quietly, but none of them felt that it was enough to live the lifestyles they felt entitled to. And none of them were fond of Albert, nor he of them.

"Brian offered to serve Charles and Debra dinner so that they might discuss the possibility of contesting their father's will.

"Charles didn't think there was much point, but Debra wanted to try, so they went. Brian served Debra and Charles a very good wine. That's the last thing I remember until I woke as this. Brian had me bury Charles and Debra's bodies.

"Then we all moved from Londinium to Calbridge and each quarter we go to the bank and sign for Brian, Charles and Debra's gold pieces and place them in the community account which Brian controls." The copy of Charles Royce looked back and forth between Pip and Yahg, which Brian controlled. "I take it he is no more."

Yahg blinked in surprise. "You take it? You are an automaton!"

"And you're an orc. How is it you even know such a word?"

Yahg almost hit him then, but didn't.

Pip said, "Answer him, Charles."

The automaton looked at her and at the dragon's claw in her hand and answered. "I don't know the details of how it works, but I have all Charles Royce's memories and the memories of my servitude. I do what I am told, but I remember more, feeling more, wanting more, caring more. I have to know what Charles knew, and I have to know what has happened since. Otherwise, I couldn't fulfill my function, but it is true my wants are not there anymore. They are memories, and less than memories."

Yahg nodded understanding.

"Who controls the money in your community account now?" Pip asked. In the back of her mind she was screaming that Brian might have been an ass, but he never would have killed his brother and sister to get their money. But she was thinking of Brian Davis, not the character Brian Royce that her ex had played in the game.

"You do," said the automaton, looking at the dragon claw key in her hand.

"How do I control it?" Pip demanded.

"How do *we* control it?" Yahg said, looking at Pip belligerently.

"She controls it through us," said Charles, just as Alvin said, "Calm down, Yahg. Pip might be tempted to loot the account and run back to the thieves' guild, but Betty's in there too. If nothing else, Betty is smart enough to know that she has a better chance of getting clear of the thieves' guild with us than without us.

"Don't you?" he asked Pip.

Pip had been thinking that she could loot the account and pay off the thieves' guild, or maybe leave the Kingdom Isles altogether. Go to the elf lands, maybe.

But Alvin's question had made her stop to think and she realized a few things. Brian Royce had lived an upper class lifestyle. He bought things, expensive things, just to have them. The twenty-four gold a year stops being a lot after you pay rent on this fairly grand townhouse, then spend several gold pieces on fancy magical items, and probably pay someone to load them. Because even if you know how, loading a magical item is exacting work, and often quite boring, so people like Brian paid others to do the loading of their magical arsenal.

He also dined out at fancy restaurants and gambled heavily. Put it all together, and Brian might well have been broke.

She looked at Alvin, then at Yahg, and said, "How much is in *our* account?"

"Five silver."

"What about debts?" Alvin asked, guessing it was going to be bad news. It was. Royce had been in debt to two money lenders to a total of fifteen gold pieces, and the debts were both past due. And these weren't people that were forgiving about money.

They woke Debra, who kept the books, and got more detail, but no real change. He owed the grocer, the haberdashery, and pretty much everyone.

* * *

They were still discussing it when Freedric arrived at the front door of the townhouse much earlier than expected. After having it explained, Freedric insisted, "We have to keep him alive."

"Why?"

"Because the only thing keeping all his creditors at bay is the belief that he will eventually pay them back. As soon as they know he's dead they'll be breaking in here to grab whatever they can. The ones that aren't going to the magistrate to seize his bank accounts."

"No. I mean why aren't you for abandoning the house and the debts and running off to build your airplane," Yagh asked.

"Because I got fired today," Freedric said. "And George Conley probably isn't going to have anything nicer to say about me than Royce did. I have my spell books, but that's about all. Unless you folks want to make another trip into the dwarven tunnels, we need to pay off Royce's debts and carefully sell off the stuff in this house.

"Making functional aircraft that are more than hang gliders is going to take money."

"It's a shame you can't ask Brian," Pip said. "The other Brian, I mean Brian Davis. I remember that when we started the game up again Brian was flush with loot from the Dwarven tunnels."

"Why can't we?" Freedric asked. By now they'd all heard Yagh's description of the event on Earth and the people getting the memories. He looked at Alvin. "Use that dream speaking and call Brian Davis."

"I never knew Brian all that well and it was thirty years ago in Tim Walter's memories.

"So contact Tim Walters," Yagh said. "Surely you remember him. Have him call Brian Davis on the phone."

Location: Houston, Texas, Merge World
Time: 2:43 PM December 31, (Merge +1)

Tim Walters was packing when he got the message from his other self. He recognized it from his memories as Alvin the Bard, so he stopped packing, laid on the bed, and closed his eyes.

Alvin the Bard: *"We need info on the Dwarven Tunnels. Contact Brian Davis."*

Tim responded, *"I need a phone number."*

The spell didn't last long. It faded after a single short exchange. Of course, a bard could cast it again and again, but it used up magical energy every time. Tim waited for a little bit, then Alvin sent him Betty Cartwright's number. *"She knows how to reach Brian Davis."*

"What's John Kipler's number? I have Jerry's."

Tim put the number in his phone, then used the spell to ask for John's number again. After all, Tim had the same spells Alvin did. He got it and put it in his phone.

Then he called Betty, only remembering the time after he'd made the call. "Hello?"

"Hello, Betty. It's Tim Walters. Sorry for calling you at work. I'm trying to get in touch with Brian. I merged with Alvin the Bard, and it's moderately important."

"I'm at work now, Tim," Betty replied, sounding like she wasn't happy.

"I understand. When is a good time to call?"

"Between five and seven," she answered, and hung up.

Then he called John Kipler. "John? Tim Walters here. I merged with Alvin the Bard and I'm pretty sure that you merged with Yagh, because I just got your number from Alvin and I assume he got it from Yagh."

There was a pause, then John answered. "Yes. Spontaneous remission, instant healing really, and green fur to go with it. But I thought he'd died. The last thing I remember is a bunch of cave cougars and Pip pointing something at us."

"I suspect the healing went both ways," Tim said. "Jerry got Freedric and I got Alvin and we're going to see if we can get the Artful Dodger to fund a space ship using magic."

"Good luck on that," John said. "Why did you call Tim?"

"Two reasons," Tim said. Even over the phone he was getting an iffy vibe from John. "I thought you might be interested in the orbit prize and I thought you might want to get in touch with the other side of your Merge."

"Not interested in either, Tim. And I have a lot of work to catch up on. Bye."

The phone went dead. "Well, that sucked," Tim muttered to himself. Then he went back to packing.

* * *

He called Betty at six thirty, five thirty Eastern. She answered on the second ring and the first thing she said was, "Please don't ever call me during work hours again."

"Sorry, Betty. When Alvin called me, I forgot about the time. Are your bosses that screwy about personal calls at work?"

"No, but no one knows I'm a Merge and I would like to keep it that way for as long as possible."

"Why?"

"Because I merged with a criminal and the *bank* I work for is hinky about hiring criminals." Then she snorted a laugh. "Outside of management, anyway."

"Right. Sorry about the timing."

"Why do you want to get in touch with Brian?"

"I don't, but Alvin the Bard does. Apparently, they are after information about what's in the dwarven tunnels near Callbridge."

"Tim, that was thirty years ago," Betty said.

"Thirty years ago for us, a couple of weeks ago for Alvin. How long ago for Pip? You have her memories?"

"I don't know. The last thing I remember is a door in the Dwarven tunnels blowing out, and me bleeding out on the floor across the hall, desperately not wanting to die."

"John Kipler remembers you pointing a wand of some sort at him and the cave cougars."

"I didn't do that." There was a pause, then, in a more thoughtful tone, Betty went on. "That must have been after the Merge. I learned about the rod of Fireballs from Brian at the end of game night. Pip had picked it up three rooms back, and failed to share it with Brian Royce because she was planning on giving it to the thieves guild to help pay off her debt. You're right, Pip's memories make it seem like it happened yesterday. But unless Brian merged with Royce, he's not likely to remember it."

"We can but try," Tim said. "But for the sake of our other selves, I think we must try."

Betty was in touch with Brian. She had two children. A girl, Vicky, who was a highschool senior and a boy Robert who was a freshman in college after taking two years to earn tuition. Both had merged. They'd played WarSpell with their father on his weekends with them. Vicky had merged with a bard and Robert with a Champion of Aganon, god of crafters. Brian was still paying child support for Vicky but had stopped making payments for Robert after he turned eighteen.

She knew about their merges, because they'd been awake playing video games when the Merge happened. They'd woken her to find out who she'd merged with. And they'd all spent the rest of last night watching the news about the Merge on TV. She picked up the phone and called Brian.

"Brian Davis."

"Hello, Brian."

"Hello, Betty. If you're calling about Vicky's child support, I'll get it to you when I can. I merged with a damn amulet wizard, but I have no amulets."

Betty held her tongue. It wouldn't do to get into a fight with Brian again. "That's not why I called," Betty thought, but didn't say, *though you're two months behind.* Instead she said, "Tim Walters called me at work today. He got a message from the other half of his Merge, a bard named Alvin."

"Got a message? How? Alvin wasn't that skilled. They started the game at third level and only gained two levels before they dropped out."

"I don't know. I haven't played a game of WarSpell in ten years. It may be a bardic spell."

"Oh yeah. That's right. It's one of the extra spells that a bard gets."

Betty thought about the rules for bards. Natural wizards get a smaller list of spells than book wizards. They get to choose three spells each time they go up a level and that's what they have. Bards get two extra spells but from a bardic list which is smaller than the Natural wizard spell list. But to get those spells they have to give up a natural wizard spell. So instead of three spells a level, a bard could get four, but only if they chose two from the bardic list.

"I remember now. Alvin had it so that he could contact me when I was in town. Tim didn't even want that spell. I insisted. I wanted a link between Alvin and Royce, because I had plans for the treasure. That's why I had you roll up Bridget the natural wizard and John roll up Simon. I wanted to keep the game going after Royce got the first treasure."

And now Betty remembered Bridget. But just as a player character she didn't have any of the additional memories for Bridget the natural wizard that she had for Pip. She didn't even know who Bridget's mother had been. But she remembered Pip's mom and they weren't joyful memories.

Brian interrupted her thoughts. "That's right, I remember now. After the fight with the cave cougars Royce went into the Dwarven Chieftain's audience chamber. I spent hours rerolling till he finally found the secret door in the ceiling of the audience chamber. Royce was such a nasty piece of work, like Gutman in The Maltese Falcon. And he'd really wanted the spell books in the dwarven Chieftain's amulet safe. I had it all planned out, the conflict between Royce and Freedric after they found the spell books.

Then Jerry got pissed over me playing Royce while being the Gamemaster at the same time. Then he and Tim quit. It ruined everything and I was just improvising after that."

"Why did you insist on playing Royce?" Betty asked, curious in spite of herself.

"Because he was such a nasty piece of work no one would have wanted to play him. Everyone wants to be the hero, not the obsessed murderer."

Betty remembered that Brian had had this grandiose plan to use the WarSpell games as a basis for novels.

"Thanks, Brian," she said and hung up.

Then she set to work recreating everything she remembered about the game. She'd give Tim a call in a couple of days when she knew what she had.

It wasn't that Betty didn't want to help. But she had two kids to take care of and bills to pay. And the stuff in that chamber was worth a lot.

CHAPTER 4: PAYING DEBTS

Location: Cloverton Counting House
Time: Morning, 10 Pago, 989AF (Merge +5)

Yahg stood at something approaching parade rest as Debra Royce, or rather the *sim* of Debra, explained that Brian had fallen while exploring caverns and wasn't healed yet. So she was here to make a payment on his loan.

"This will barely pay the interest," complained John Cloverton.

"Actually, it will pay the interest owed and five silver of the principle," Debra replied, having been briefed by Pip who had gone over Brian Royce's books and the loan agreement, using Betty's memories of accounting.

"There is the penalty."

"There is nothing in the contract about a penalty," Debra said. "You had the option to call in the debt once it was past due, but having failed to do so, you may not arbitrarily add penalties."

"It's the way things are done."

"Perhaps, but it is not the law."

"Then be assured the next time your brother is late, we shall call in the debt." Cloverton leaned forward threateningly and Yahg grunted and put his hand on the hilt of his sword.

"There will be no more late payments," Debra said without paying attention to either Cloverton's threat or Yahg's response.

Location: Royce Townhouse, Callbridge
Time: Morning, 10 Pago, 989AF (Merge +5)

Freedric visualized a purple swirl, then carefully placed it in the Z-rocks, while Pip looked on. It turned out that Pip didn't know how to load magical items, but she did want to learn. So Freedric was teaching her starting with the Z-rocks. The Z-rocks were three rocks, a jet rock and two amber ends. If you looked at them at the right angle, they looked rather like a z. They were also a pun on Xerox, as Freedric knew from Jerry's memories. When the spell had been crafted into the Z-rocks, you placed the item on a sheet of paper, invoked the item, and pulled the item evenly down the sheet that had writing or pretty much anything on it. Then you pulled the Z-rocks down a blank piece of paper and the image was copied onto the second sheet.

In the process of teaching Pip, he was loading the Z-rocks so that he could copy a page of one of the books on the making of magical items that Royce had in his collection. Freedric realized that the Z-rocks item could have been modified only slightly to allow you to make two or ten copies of a given page, rather than the one. But it would require making a new magical item and letting it age for a couple of years before its first use.

With the help of the *sims* and a bit of time, they'd gotten access to Royce's workshop and magic safe. And they'd spent the last few days selling off the wealth in the townhouse to pay down the debts, both Pip's and Royce's.

Alvin had stayed in touch with Tim, so they knew that Jerry and Tim were planning to try to start a company to use magic to get into space.

Freedric wished them well. However, Tim hadn't heard back from Betty Cartwright and Pip was arguing against pushing the matter. That would just make Betty stubborn.

Having finished loading the Z-rocks, Freedric copied another page and then watched as Pip loaded it, correcting her when the magic indicated she wasn't visualizing things quite right.

They kept at it for most of the morning, then they both needed a break.

After lunch, Freedric spent an hour going over his designs for a small airplane. They were changing every time he looked at them. The addition of magic changed everything and nothing. It was still an issue of how to get into the air and use a wing to convert forward motion into lift, but the forward motion could be achieved in too many ways. Electric motors powered by magic batteries. Magic motors that spun on their own or magic on the wings and fuselage of the plane that pushed it forward. Freedric was even considering abandoning magic altogether, except to make the parts of an internal combustion engine that would run on gasoline, or possibly oil of some sort.

Electric engines would make Short Take Off and Landing or Vertical Take Off and Landing a lot easier, but that would almost require computers. And they didn't have computers.

* * *

The four of them were having dinner talking about the projects. Freedric asked Alvin, "How long would it take you to make a really efficient electric motor."

"Not long," Alvin said with a smile. "Two, maybe three years."

Yahg laughed and Pip giggled.

Freedric didn't throw a dinner roll at Alvin, but he very much wanted to. Instead he asked, "Explain please?"

"First, I have to make the magnets. Understand these aren't chunks of iron heated red hot and exposed to a magnetic field. That's fine for a compass needle, but not for the sort of very strong magnets you need for an efficient electric motor. For that you need rare earth magnets, probably Neodymium, made and magnetized in a *very* strong magnetic field. Then you have to make the electromagnets. There we have a little luck. A few years ago, the way to do it would be coils of really thin copper wire, insulated and wound together. So we'd have to hand wind the insulated wires. Recently, a new way of doing it was invented. They are called hairpin motors, because the little copper bits look like hairpins. They are plugged and welded into sockets. Of course, you need a computer to control when they are turned off and—"

"You weren't here when I asked him about semiconductors," Yagh interrupted. "Twenty years, he says. First, we have to create the chemical industry to make silicon wafers, then the doping. And on and on. Getting Tim Walters' memories has turned our good Alvin into a pessimist of the worst sort."

"What sort is that?" Pip asked.

"One who's right," Yagh explained in disgust.

Location: San Francisco California, Merge world
Time: 9:33 PM January 5, (Merge +6)

Tim Walters answered his phone. It was Betty Cartwright, "Hi, Betty," Tim said distractedly. He was looking through files that Jerry had been working on in preparation for today's meeting with the Dodger. He hoped that Honey Abrams would agree and he hoped that Dodger was right about her abilities, but he wasn't sure of either, and so wasn't paying a lot of attention to Betty or her situation. "Have you found out where the magic vault is located?"

"I think so. But what's in it for me?"

That was a shock, and yet it wasn't. It wasn't something that Tim would have expected from Betty, but it was very much something that Alvin would expect from Pip. It was enough to put the electrical engineer very much on the back burner while Alvin the bard came to the forefront. "I don't know, Betty. What do you want, and how do you expect Pip to pay you? Neither of you can do more than speak indirectly to each other, through me and Alvin the Bard."

"I know that, Tim. I've been worrying about it for the past three days, but I have a daughter in highschool and a son in college and I'm probably going to lose my job when the bank finds out I merged with a criminal."

"What do you gain by withholding the information, Betty, other than bad blood down the road? What was Pip's situation last you remember? What would cause her to go back into the Dwarven Tunnels after that adventure where Freedric and Alvin quit? Jerry and I quit because the game wasn't all that fun and Brian was playing fast and loose with his role as Gamemaster, but Freedric and Alvin quit because those tunnels are bloody dangerous."

"The thieves' guild was going to kill her," Betty admitted reluctantly.

"Do you want to be responsible for Pip's death when you could have provided the knowledge that would have saved her? "Look, Betty, Jerry and I are out here in California trying to set up something in the aerospace industry. We don't know if it's going to happen, but if it does and I'm in a position to do so, and you end up losing your job, I'll try to get you on with the new company."

"That's a lot of ands, Alvin," Betty said. "Sorry, Tim, but you sounded a lot like Alvin just then."

"I probably did. I have his memories as well as my own. Look, Betty. I don't have any advantage from this either. I'm going to be spending some magic for no real gain to get what you tell me to Alvin. But our other selves are stuck in that game world and I'd like to help them out if I can. Any cost to you, any effort you put out, has already happened. You might as well put it to use."

Betty agreed rather grudgingly. She got Tim's email and sent him some files.

* * *

Betty's attitude hadn't made Tim want to help her, but the work in the files suggested that she might be very useful. It was detailed, precise and clear. Now all Tim had to do was figure out how to put it into words, so that Alvin and the rest would understand. It took several castings of the spell over several days, but he got it.

Location: Royce Townhouse, Callbridge
Time: Morning, 15 Pago, 989AF (Merge +10)

Pip was loading the Z-rocks to copy another page, but that didn't take her entire concentration. It left her plenty of mental energy to spend on missing her kids. More accurately, she missed Betty Cartwright's kids, but she remembered them as *her* kids. She remembered giving birth to them and feeding them and watching as they grew into people. She rather desperately wanted to sit at the dinner table and listen to her daughter go on about the boy she was attracted to this week.

She also missed air conditioning, chocolate cake, her car, and books. Lots and lots of books on her ereader. Surprisingly, she also missed politics, as much as they had disgusted her in her life as Betty Cartwright.

No, that wasn't quite right. Pip missed, rather desperately, the thing she had taken for granted her entire life as Betty Cartwright. She missed a government that was answerable to the citizenry it governed.

The government of the Kingdom Isles wasn't. It wasn't answerable to any one of Pip's class. All the answering went the other way.

She finished loading the Z-rocks and started asking the sim of Debra Royce about the government of the Kingdom Isles. Pip had never known much about the government here, and Betty knew even less. Just that it was a monarchy with characteristics of feudalism.

Debra, or rather Debra's sim, did know quite a bit. She had lived among that class of gentry. Pip listened as Debra's sim described her life. The parties, the knights and compared it to what she'd read as Betty Cartwright. There was a Parliament, a House of Lords, and a House of Commons. In fact, Albert was often elected to the Commons, just as their father had been.

But the people who selected the members of Parliament were all landed. All gentry, at the least. There was literally no one in the Kingdom Isles who was responsible to Pip, or all the Pips in Callbridge, be they thief, butcher, baker, or candlestick maker.

And Pip was starting to get angry about that. It wasn't a loud anger. Both Pip and Betty were much too pragmatic for that sort of anger, but it was slowly turning into a really hard anger.

The sort of anger that starts revolutions.

She called in Yahg and he was unimpressed. He didn't disagree. He just didn't think that there was anything that they could do about it. The absolute best they could hope for was a better life for themselves and maybe for their families. "Face it, Pip. This is the 13th, maybe the 14th century. Knights in shining armor and us peasant types keep our place or get our backs bloodied at best, or hung up on a gibbet."

She tried the same conversation with Alvin, and while he was more sympathetic than Yahg, he didn't see any good options either.

Freedric had a vote. Well, Freedric's father, who was a property owner in Londinium, had a vote. And Freedric, as a licensed book wizard, might aspire to the property requirements that might let him vote for the members of Parliament from Callbridge. All two of them.

"But I agree with you, Pip. So far we've done nothing but plan to improve our own condition." He glanced over at Yahg. "Nothing wrong with that, but we should at least be looking for ways to improve the lot of . . ."

"I believe the word you're looking for," Yahg said sardonically, "is proletariat."

"I don't remember John Kipler being quite the cynic you are, Yahg."

"Oh, he was," Yahg said. "Even when you knew him, and it got worse as his condition got worse. By the time of the Merge, John didn't believe in much of anything. In a way, I'm actually more in sympathy with Pip here than John would be. I, at least, want my parents and my little brother and sister to have a better life."

"I want that too," Pip said. "For your family and all the other families in the Kingdom Isles, orc or human."

"Fine, Pip. You figure out a way to get my family included, and I'll do what I can to help. It's a safe bet because no orc has even gotten a knighthood, much less a noble title. Nor even been allowed to own the property that would allow them to vote."

"I'll take that as your word, Yahg," Pip said, "and I *will* find a way to get the vote even for orcs." In spite of her lofty promise, Pip had no clue how it might be done. Not then.

Location: Royce Townhouse, Callbridge
Time: Morning, 17 Pago, 989AF (Merge +12)

Alvin was a musician, not an artist, and though Tim had taken drafting courses in college, they'd been CAD courses. The drawings of the Dwarven tunnels were *really* bad. Still, when combined with the description, Freedric was able to do some decent drawings. A book wizard had to be able to draw in order to record spells. They'd gone over the drawings and notes in detail to determine where to go and where to avoid.

The legal creditors were at bay for the moment, but Pip was still in a great deal of trouble. So a trip to the dwarven tunnels to get saleable magical items was necessary.

* * *

The good news was that between Betty Cartwright and Brian Davis' old notes, they had a pretty solid image of what was in the tunnels. Better yet, the Dwarf clan chief's magical item safe was located just off the cave cougar room. They hadn't found it because Yahg wasn't adept at traps and hidden passages and because the Dwarf clan chief had been clever. People, especially dwarves, tend to look for doors and passages at ground level or at least on walls.

The clan chief had put the amulet safe in a room that could only be accessed through the ceiling of the room below it. That room was the room with the fireball trapped door that the cave cougars had occupied. It had been the clan chief's council room and was twice as tall as the surrounding rooms.

Freedric looked around the dining room in Royce House, and got nods all around. "Tonight then?"

Location: Leaving Callbridge
Time: Just Past Sunset, 17 Pago, 989AF

Pip was feeling the hairs on the back of her neck lift and she wasn't at all sure why. Nor was she sure what to do about it. Before the Merge, Pip didn't trust anyone, and would have kept her own council. She would have looked for a way to slip away from the party, to make sure that whatever it was, landed on them and missed her.

But Betty was a bit more trusting than Pip, and a lot more caring of her companions. It was having an effect. The fact that Freedric and Yahg both now knew she was a girl, and neither of them had tried to force her, or hit on her, had left her a lot more trusting of them. Companions you could trust were worth more than companions you couldn't. She stepped up her pace a little until she was between Yahg and Alvin.

"Something's wrong," she said quietly.

They were less than two miles from the entrance to the tunnels.

Yahg stretched, then said not particularly loudly, "We've miles to go and I didn't get a lot of rest today. Let's stop for a bit."

"We should go on. We have a distance to cover before we get there," Alvin complained, looking around not as casually as he was trying to appear.

Freedric, from a little behind said, "If we're going to stop, I want to craft a spare wizard bolt. It shouldn't take long."

* * *

They stopped and Freedric pulled out his books. "Pip, sit here. I want to show you this."

Pip was immediately nervous. Was he about to try something after all? But no. That wasn't Freedric's way, nor Jerry Garman's.

She sat next to him, still ready to bolt, and Freedric took a stylus from his pack and scratched into the bare earth.

Crafting Hide in Shadows?

Then she understood. Freedric had a second level spell called hide in shadows. It didn't make you invisible or work in bright light, but in evening or at night, it did a good job of keeping you unseen. She nodded and watched as he crafted the spell, flipping between pages of his spellbook.

Yahg had laid on the ground and started to snore as soon as they'd stopped, and Alvin was playing his lute.

The lute playing was also a spell, and a fairly subtle one. If a bard played it while people around him were resting, the effect was to let them have four times the rest. The bard, of course, didn't get any rest while he was playing, but a party could use it and the bard could then rest while the rest of the party split up the watches, and everyone would be well rested the next morning.

* * *

Thirty minutes later, Freedric had crafted the spell and Pip slipped out of the camp to do her business and effectively disappeared.

It took her fifteen minutes to find the followers. She hid in the shadows and listened as they argued about what to do.

"We should grab them now and beat it out of them," said George the Touch. George was clumsy and had early on tried his hand as a cut purse, but he couldn't cut a purse without getting caught. But he could beat the person who caught him to death. That he could do. All of them were like that. They were muggers and extorters, not a second story man or pick pocket in the bunch.

All were members of the thieves guild and they wouldn't be here, not that many, not without the agreement of the council of thieves. That was when Pip realized that the guild of thieves had no intention of letting her live, dues paid or not. In one way, it was a shock because she'd spent her life in the guild. Her mother had been a member and had sold her to the guild when she was eight. The guild had taught her and used her. They were her clan, the group who commanded what little loyalty Pip offered anyone. Believing they would kill her was hard.

At the same time, Pip was fairly bright, brighter now that she had Betty's knowledge and memories. Knowing the politics of the guild, she'd been more than half expecting it. There was a struggle going on in the guild between the thieves and the thugs. A cutpurse or a second story man, even a grifter, lived by skill and wit. A thug just took. And the fight between the thieves and the thugs was ongoing. It looked like the thugs were making a play for dominance and the thieves on the council were going along.

Alvin, though not a member of the guild, operated on the edges of it, so knew about the politics and they'd spoken of it. Yahg was a member of the guild even though in game terms he'd been a warrior, not a criminal. Before the Merge, Yahg had been a thug and Pip didn't understand why the thugs following them hadn't warned him. Then she wondered if they had.

Curly Joe said, "You think we'll have to kill Yahg?"

"He didn't tell the council where Pip was staying," said Brass Balls. "That means he's working for Royce, and disobeyed the council to do it."

"He's a tough bastard," George said. "I don't want to be the one to try to take him."

Squirrely Sam held up a crossbow. "I'll do for Yahg. The damn orc never should have been let in the guild." Squirrely Sam hated everyone that wasn't pure human. Orcs, elves, dwarves, lizardmen, it didn't matter. If they weren't pure human, they weren't people, and he hated half breeds even more.

"Drop it," said Brass Balls. "We're doing it the way we were told. We follow them until they find the magic safe and then we kill them and take it. Once they're gone, Royce gets his through the law courts."

Quietly, Pip slipped away and back to camp. Still quietly, with Alvin's help, she let Freedric and Yahg know what was happening.

John Kipler was *a lot* smarter than Yahg. He'd also been playing strategy games since he was ten years old and he'd been approaching sixty when he merged with Yahg. He, too, wondered why the brute force faction of the thieves guild had failed to warn him. After consideration, he still wasn't sure. Either someone had noticed that he was smarter than he had been, or they just didn't care about killing one of their own. On the other hand, the fact of Squirrely Sam with the crossbow meant that he no longer owed the thieves' guild anything.

He'd gone over the maps and descriptions from Betty and Brian's memory and files. And he had a good idea of what was where in the Dwarven tunnels.

It was Yahg's plan they used.

Location: Wetfang Village, near Callbridge
Time: Two Hours Past Sunset, 17 Pago, 989AF

Quietly, but under observation, Pip led them into the root cellar of a small farming village. Yahg was last and, "clumsy lout that he was," he left a clear boot print next to the hidden entrance to the Dwarven tunnels. Worse, he left the hidden entrance not quite closed.

They knew their way. They had both their prior experience and the maps provided by way of Tim and Alvin. Since they were underground, they didn't try to be all that quiet. But when they got to the corridor that would have taken them to the amulet safe, they took a right turn rather than the left turn that would take them to the treasure.

Two more turns and they were at a pressure plate, one that they wouldn't have known about save for Betty. They didn't step on it. They hopped over it. Then they went on about twenty feet, turned another corner and waited.

* * *

The group that followed them were using torches, not the magic light on the top of Royce's staff. What Pip, knowing what to look for in the clear light of the staff, had found easily, the followers didn't see at all.

They stepped on the pressure plate and a fireball bloomed among them.

Then Pip, in a rage at the betrayal by the only family she'd ever known, stepped out into the tunnel and emptied the rod of fireballs into them.

There had been a total of seven toughs. Plenty to take down a thief, an incompetent wizard, a bard, and a single warrior, who if he was a tough fighter, was known to be an idiot.

Fireballs are mostly flames, but some blast. They do a lot of damage. By the time Freedric stepped out of the side passage there was nothing for him to do but be sick from the smell of cooked human.

"What do we do with the bodies?" Yahg asked casually.

"Nothing," Pip said. "Leave them here. They won't be found."

"I know and that's the problem," Yahg said. "The guild knows it sent them to rob us and kill us. We come back and they don't, the guild is going to assume we killed them, and charge us for their deaths."

"That's ridiculous," Freedric said.

"That's how the guild works," Pip said. "If you're going to steal from another member of the guild, you'd better get permission first."

"They had permission. We didn't," Yahg said. "At least we have to assume that they had permission."

"But we didn't rob them."

"I know, but who is going to believe that?" Yahg said.

"There's nothing we can do about it," Pip said.

"There may be," Yahg said. Then he looked around the group. "It will need Alvin at his most persuasive, but we might be able to square ourselves with the guild, and put one in the eye of the thugs at the same time."

"I like the sound of that," Alvin said.

"So do I," Pip agreed. They all looked at Freedric.

Freedric was a scholar. He didn't travel in those circles. He didn't *want* to travel in those circles. And the addition of Jerry Garman's memories didn't change that. Jerry was an aeronautical engineer, a designer of things more than a maker of them. One thing he very much wasn't was any sort of mobster. "I don't see how I can help. I'm not saying you're wrong. I'm not disapproving. I'm certainly not going to call the cops. But I couldn't get a lie past the village idiot."

Alvin laughed. "That, my friend, is very true. So Freedric will stay in the town house working on his design and being our wizard in reserve. Or do you have something else in mind, Yahg?"

"What I have in mind is something close to that," Yahg said. "Brian Royce was a skilled amulet wizard. He made magical items as well as loading them when he wasn't hiring others to load them. We need to keep him alive but hole up in the townhouse while he heals from the injuries he suffered in his last trip." Yahg pointed to the floor. "Here."

"I can do that for now," Freedric agreed, "but eventually we are going to have to let him die."

"Yes," Yahg agreed, "but not until all debts with the guild of thieves are settled. Until then, more than his magic, we need the wealth and civic prominence he had as a shield."

Following Yahg's plan, they stripped the bodies of anything they could and put it all in a pack. While they were doing that, Yahg explained.

"Our story is simple. We didn't know anything until we heard the fire ball go off behind us. We had spotted the pressure plate and avoided it. Pip was working on a door around the corner when we heard the blast, came back and found them dead. How is anyone going to tell if they were killed by one fire ball or four?" He grinned a grin that Freedric thought might give him nightmares, then continued. "Pip and Alvin then realized what was going on and we collected up their gear. Not for ourselves. We're loyal members of the guild. No, we collected it up to return it to the guild and lodge a complaint about their actions."

"Because," Alvin said, nodding, "they can't have had the thieves guild's permission to rob us when Pip and Yahg are members in good standing of the guild."

CHAPTER 5: THE GUILD OF THIEVES

Location: Dwarven Tunnels under Wetfang
Time: Just past Midnight, 18 Pago, 989AF

After that, the rest of the night was fairly straightforward. Using Alvin's Lift spell, Pip was levitated to the ceiling and found the hidden panel that unlatched the amulet safe. Then she was lifted into it and dropped a rope for the rest to climb.

The amulet safe was a small room, ten feet by fifteen. Its walls were lined with shelves that were mostly empty. What the Dwarves had left when they were escaping were just the most recently made and least stable of magical items.

They found and collected 36 magical items. Including 2 permanent dwarven ax heads, 2 sets permanent vambraces of armor, 4 permanent dwarven swords, 10 permanent light crystals, 6 permanent combs of cleaning, 3 permanent amulets of servant, 2 permanent stone shovels, 4 permanent chisels of stone shaping, 1 everfull cask of water, 2 permanent bags of holding.

Everything in the amulet safe that was magical was permanent. The reason was a function of the design of the WarSpell game and the history of the Dwarven Empire centered on the caverns of Rime and often called the Rimen Empire.

Dwarfs are makers, not artists or scholars. There are, of course, exceptions but in general dwarfs are more comfortable putting their magic into an item, than putting it in themselves which, one way or another, intercessors, book and natural wizards all do.

The thing about magical items and amulets is, they need to be aged and the longer they are aged before they are put to their first use, the more powerful and easier to load they become. Eventually, if they are left long enough, they start to load themselves. The Dwarven empire had been thrown out of this part of the Kingdom Isles well before the Fall of Rime. So these magical items had been made, and placed in the amulet safe to age, hundreds of years ago.

In the normal course of events, they would have been left in the amulet safe a few months, a couple of years, maybe even a decade. Dwarfs were long lived after all. Then they would have been taken out of the safe, activated, and been perfectly normal magical items. Normal magical items hold a spell for a few days or weeks, depending on how long they were aged. If the spell is used in that time, the magical item is then ready to be reloaded. If not, after a while the spell decays and a new spell has to be placed in it before it can be used.

In this case, the Dwarves had been driven out by the barbarian humans and most of them killed. So items that would have, in the normal course of business, been left to age for a few years or at most a couple of decades, had been left sitting for centuries instead.

By the time they were found by the four merged adventurers, they were *all* self recharging or continuous items.

It was a great find, assuming they could find someone to buy them. But to Freedric, they were almost insignificant compared to the other thing he found.

Dwarven spell books. This was what Royce had been after, the thing he'd been obsessed with. Royce's Maltese Falcon.

It's true that Dwarven wizards are usually amulet wizards. That doesn't mean that they aren't skilled. While the difference between a book wizard and an amulet wizard is very sharp and distinct in the rules of the game, the difference is a lot more vague and multi-valued when you're living in a game world.

A spell meant for a magical item can't be directly used by a book wizard as a crafted spell. It has to be modified. But, the instructions to load an amulet of servant, will get a book wizard eighty percent of the way to a servant spell that a book wizard can craft and carry around with him, until he needs to have his socks darned.

More importantly if Freedric was going to be building airplanes than what he needed was amulet magic. Spells that he could load into the body of the plane. These books were references to do that.

Then the first thing they did was take each item one at a time out of the spell safe and activate it. First in line were the two bags of holding. They would need those to hold the rest of their loot.

Then the amber jewels of light. By now each of them produced the light of a sunny day.

Then the vambraces of Armor. They went to Alvin and Pip. They were made of mithril and shined silvery till they were put on then became translucent. They were light and flexible but gave the protection of full plate armor. The dwarven swords were based on the Roman gladius. From the notes they had from Brian Davis they knew that these ranged from plus 35 to plus 45 or in D&D terms they were all plus 4. They would keep those in case they needed them. The rest of the items they would try to carefully sell.

They would have to be careful because these were the sort of items that would attract the attention of the authorities. And the various knights, barons, counts, earls, dukes and princes of the Kingdom Isles were all different in every way but one. They were all greedy as heck and eager to do adventurers out of their loot.

Location: Royce Townhouse, Callbridge
Time: Just After Dawn, 18 Pago, 989AF

Pip had scouted for other members of the Thieves Guild and hadn't found any. They all hoped the Guild was still unaware of the precise location of the Dwarven tunnels. Meanwhile, it had been a long and exhausting night and Freedric wanted nothing more than to go to bed in the guest room he'd co-opted. Instead, he spent an hour storing everything that they'd gotten from the amulet safe. None of them would be using them for now. Meanwhile Yahg, Pip, and Alvin went to the Thieves guild.

Location: Mortemer's Tavern and Trinkets
Time: Just Approaching Noon, 18 Pago, 989AF

Alvin knocked on the door of the Tavern and shop. The building was moderately large, two stories tall, made of oak and wattle and daub. The front part of the ground floor was a tavern, and about half the back was a pawnshop. There were rooms on the second floor, and behind the counter in the pawnshop, was a trap door that went into the sewer system of Callbridge.

The peephole in the door opened and a gruff voice said, "We're closed." The peephole started to close and Alvin said, "Pinta sent me."

There was no one named Pinta. Pinta was Dwarvish for five and referred to the five members of the council of thieves. Of whom one had died two months ago and a replacement had yet to be named.

"Who told you that, minstrel?" The voice sounded quite angry now.

"Open the door and find out," Alvin said. There were several codes that might cause this door to open. Some meant you had goods to sell to the fence. Some that you had money to buy something the guild offered, or were here to pay a debt. Like the debt Pip owed. But this one was the one you used if you were bringing a complaint to the thieves guild council.

The peephole closed and the door opened, then Yahg and Pip stepped to where they could see and be seen.

The man in the doorway needed a shave. Not that it would help much. He had a scar from his right eye to the point of his chin, and the eye was missing. There was no patch, just a hole.

Yahg stepped up to the door guard and the guard stepped back.

Yahg was six feet tall and heavy with green fur and a very orcish look for a half orc. Alvin and Pip followed him in.

The thieves guild kept odd hours, but the council tended to start their day around noon and end it by ten.

At the moment, they were having breakfast in the main room of the tavern part of the building.

They were at a long table in the corner of the room. The table was placed so that all the counsel members had their backs to the wall. It wasn't the sort of place and these weren't the sort of people who would sit with their backs to a door or window.

There was one woman and three men. The woman looked at Yahg and asked, "What did you do to Squirrely Sam?"

"Nothing," Yahg said.

Then before he could say anything else Alvin interrupted. "I assume Squirrely Sam was one of the gentlemen you sent to rob members of the guild?" Not waiting for an answer, he continued. "If so, he was dead when we found him in the Tunnels. Yahg, put the gear on the table."

Yahg emptied a heavy sack containing knives, swords, blackjacks, bits of armor, a scorched and broken crossbow, and other odds and ends including a pendant and three rings onto the table while Alvin continued to speak.

"We were investigating the tunnels that Brian Royce found when we heard an explosion. We went to investigate and by the time we reached them every one of the fellows who were apparently sent to follow us was quite dead. A fireball spell will do that. This isn't the first of those traps we've found in the dwarven tunnels nor the second.

"Now as honorable and upright members of the guild, Yahg and Pip are here to report the unfortunate demise of their fellow guild members and ask this council what they were doing following us into tunnels that were no part of the guild's affairs?"

The council normally had five members, and that had been the case until a few months ago. Three of them had been among the thieves faction and two among the toughs faction. Then Tom the Lockpick had died under mysterious circumstances and a new fifth member had not yet been chosen.

Callbridge was a fair size town, having a university and several shops, as well as a decent river fishing industry. A total population of perhaps eighteen thousand people, making it the third largest city on the Isle of Wiles and the fifth in the Kingdom Isles. It had a variety of criminal enterprises and the thieves guild oversaw much of the crime in the city. In spite of that there were less than two hundred members of the thieves guild. The council more reigned than ruled over the guild. The loss of seven toughs who had died trying to rob and kill Yahg and Pip was a serious blow to Mack the Cudgel because they answered to him.

Alvin could tell that Mack wasn't happy. On the other hand, Pete the Cat seemed pleased, though he was trying to hide it.

Maggs, the woman on the council, was looking ambivalent and Tommy the Black was looking almost as pissed as Mack.

"I should add that Mister Royce isn't happy with Pip, Yahg, or me right now. Half the reason he included us was to make sure that the guild stayed out. He's now considering other means to the same end. And I would remind you that Royce is a wealthy man with connections in Londinium. The sort of man who can call down the kind of official displeasure that the guild can't afford."

Alvin left the rest unsaid. If they'd all died in the tunnels it wouldn't have meant much. In fact, many of the wealthy of Callbridge would have been privately pleased. But the guild missed, and a live Brian Royce could make them pay, if they didn't make amends.

"Which is why you're here," Pete the Cat said, with a half smile. "What sort of recompense does Master Royce want from the guild?"

"He wants you to back off while we search the dwarven tunnels," Alvin said. "Look, Royce is obsessed with a set of dwarven magic books. Books on the design and manufacture of dwarven magical items. The sort of stuff they used to make their tunnels and to keep them well lit and with drinkable water. The stuff they used to mine the mid-Centriaum mountain range. He thinks it's in those tunnels somewhere."

Now Alvin had their interest. But Maggs wasn't looking as greedy as the rest. "What do you think, player?" she asked.

"I doubt it," Alvin admitted candidly. "I suspect that there may be magic books all right, but they aren't the dwarven philosopher's stone Royce wants them to be. I'd guess that if the dwarves did leave any magical items in their amulet safes, they'll be worth a lot. But at this point, even if we do find something, it's going to be really hard to get him to bring them to you. He'll be afraid you'll just take them and kill him."

"Not an unreasonable fear," Pete said with a look at Mack the Cudgel.

"What about Pip?" Tommy the Black demanded. "She owes." It was one of Tommy's people who'd gotten killed by the city guard. Pip had run away across the rooftops without stopping to give warning.

"I'll pay," Pip said. "I would have been here to pay now, if you hadn't sent them—" She pointed at the items on the table. "—to kill us."

"Don't try to tell me," Tommy pointed at his chest with a thumb. "You stopped hunting for treasure to bring us word of the death of guild members."

"No," Alvin said before Pip could say something stupid. "But Royce called a halt as soon as we found them. He wanted to make sure that there weren't any more hiding outside the barn." Alvin didn't pay any overt attention to the expressions on their faces as he gave them that misleading piece of information.

He didn't need to. Yahg had John Kipler's memories and intelligence, but everyone thought he was still the dumb half-orc that he had been. So while Alvin talked, Yahg watched and listened for reactions, looking dumb and uninterested.

They got a month.

Location: Royce Townhouse, Callbridge
Time: Near Sunset, 18 Pago, 989AF (Merge +13)

After sleeping most of the day, Freedric woke and went down to the dining room to a quiet argument between Pip and Yahg. Alvin had gone up to his room to rest.

"We have to sell them," Pip said.

"We need them," Yahg answered.

"What are you—" Freedric yawned hugely. "Excuse me. What are you arguing about?"

"The stone shovels," Pip answered.

"Oh." Freedric remembered the dull stone shovel heads they'd found in the tunnels. "What are they?"

"They turn stone into mud, then back into stone as soon as the mud leaves the shovel."

That was a clever notion, Freedric conceded, especially if you had a form of some sort to put the temporary mud into. Even more if the stone bonded to the stone already in the form. You dig a hole in a granite cliff face, and use the "mud" to make a granite wall. Still, even the permanent ones weren't going to be able to compete with a truck full of concrete. Not that there were trucks full of concrete yet, but there would be. Someday.

"We should sell them," Freedric said. "Pip's right."

"We can use them to expand the basement," Yahg insisted. "Dig an internal well. There's an aqueduct sixty feet down. And dig a passage to the sewers."

"Do you want to dig it?" Freedric asked. "I sure don't."

"Do you want to find someone who will buy them, no questions asked?" Yahg asked in turn.

"Good point. I wouldn't have a clue where to start. How did things go at the guild?"

"About as we expected," Yahg said. "Tommy the Black wants Pip dead, whatever the rest of the council thinks, and Mack the Cudgel wants us all dead. But I think that Mack's in trouble, and Maggs may well be looking for a way to cut him off at the knees.

"Tom the Lockpick's death gave the thugs the upper hand in the council. They've always had more muscle, but the thieves used to have better connections. A lot of those connections were through old Tom."

Freedric went to the dining table and sat. One of the servants came over when he sat and he said, "Bring me some stew." There was always stew in the kitchen. In a few moments, he had a bowl, a spoon, and half a small loaf of bread. The stew had more beans than pork, but it was a step up from what he'd been eating in the small room he'd rented. "I've been trying almost from the beginning to find a way to get us separated from the guild, but everything we do seems to pull us back in.

"We need another avenue of disposing of the goods from the tunnels." Freedric thought of his family. They were moderately well off in Londinium. His father was a solicitor on the staff of the Lord Mayor, but lacked the connections to move goods of questionable pedigree, and would probably call the Lord Mayor's constables if Freedric were to show up on his doorstep with a load of dwarven magical items. Pip and Yahg's parents were less help, and Alvin's family were tenant farmers on an estate in Northern Skutes. No help there.

Then he had a thought.

"Pip, please wake Debra," Freedric said.

Pip wasn't comfortable around Debra. Debra wasn't a person, but very much seemed like a person, and that freaked Pip out. Well, it freaked Freedric out a bit too, but this was important.

* * *

A few minutes later, he had the *sim* of Debra sit at the table and asked her about her brother, Albert. "What is he like, and why does he dislike you?"

"Albert was always to be the heir. There was nothing anyone could do about that, and he knew it. He was a spoiled primadonna when we were children, and then he went off to boarding school. When he came back, he was worse. Nothing any of us did was worthwhile."

"Was he right?"

"Mostly. By the time our father died, we were acting out just to embarrass Albert. Charles was the worst, but Brian and I . . ." The *sim* shook its head in a fairly convincing show of embarrassment. "All of us were pretty bad. Brian was the least belligerent. He was father's favorite. We all despised him, and I think he hated Charles and Debra more than he hated Albert. Albert's only complaint about Brian was that he spent too much on his magical items. When father died, Albert claimed all of Brian's toys were the family's and sold them. That was why Debra thought that Brian might have a scheme to get their money from Albert."

"So Albert would have the connections to sell magical items?" Freedric asked.

"I assume so," said the *sim*.

"Using your knowledge of Albert, how would he react to a package containing a permanent stone shovel and assuring him that there would be more if payments were made to your account in the bank?"

"He'd short me on the gold to be paid and insist that I owed it to the family, but if he knew there would only be more coming if I got paid for the first, he'd pay."

Pip and Yahg had been watching this and now Pip asked a question. "How much would he short you?"

"I don't know. Maybe half what he got for the item."

"That's more than the guild would pay."

They spent the rest of the evening working out what the note would say in consultation with the *sims* of Debra and Charles.

Then they sent off the package with one shovel to Albert with the letter written in such a way as to persuade Albert that Debra was stealing the items from Brian and if she was found out, there would be no more.

CHAPTER 6: FINANCES IN PLACE

Location: Royce Townhouse, Callbridge
Time: Near Sunset, 28 Pago, 989AF

Yagh and the *sim* of Debra returned from the bank with five gold. The shovel had sold, they knew, for ten. Albert reported that he was keeping one gold as agent's commission, and sent the other nine to Debra. He hoped it would help and yes, he was in a position to sell other items for her, should she have them. The letter went on.

I regret the manner of our parting. I cannot approve of your choices while you were living in our townhouse in Londinium, but I hold no ill will to you or our brothers.

Please keep in touch, whether you have more goods for me to dispose of or not.

Along with the note was a receipt for ten gold from a respected dealer in dwarven antiquities in Londinium. The five gold were given to Pip and she and Yagh went to the thieves guild to pay down her debt.

The fact that they got the money not by robbing someone or burgling a house was noted. They were being watched by the guild. They knew that. Meanwhile, Yagh had, over the last ten days, used the second stone shovel to dig a passage from the basement of the townhouse to a sewer that ran under a Callbridge street. Then, using one of the chisels of stone shaping, he camouflaged the exit. In that way they could slip out of the townhouse without being seen by the guild.

There was one other effect. The money coming from Londinium increased the belief in the guild that Brian Royce had powerful or at least wealthy connections in Londinium. Also that he was still alive and in a position to call on those connections.

The next load to Albert included two of the chisels of stone shaping and a dwarven ax head.

Then Freedric and the *sim* of Charles contacted Royce's solicitor and set up a new company for the construction of magical crafts. Ownership in the company included Charles, Debra, Freedric, Yahg, and Pip.

Location: Royce Townhouse, Callbridge
Time: A Little After Sunset, 10 Wovoro, 989AF

The next money from Albert had arrived yesterday and Pip and Yahg had paid another installment on Pip's debt to the guild. Also, much of Brian Royce's debts to the merchants of Callbridge had been cleared. They still owed money, and Pip and Yahg had agreed to the airplane project. Alvin had been in favor from the beginning. They could clear Brian Royce's and Pip's debts from what they'd found in the amulet safe, but there were more treasures in the tunnels, and Tim had been in touch with Alvin about where and what sort of traps there were.

Betty had lost her job at the bank when they found out she was merged with a criminal, but Tim had gotten her on with S.ex. Inc. They were getting ready to move to Houston. As for Brian Davis, Betty and the kids had gone to visit and gone through his notes with a fine-tooth comb.

They now had a complete list of the traps and monsters in the tunnels as well as the locations of the treasures.

They went down into the basement and used the secret passage to reach the sewers, then followed the sewers for three blocks and came up well away from the townhouse.

It was a careful trip to the dwarven tunnels and the armor shop. The armor was less magical, but still worth a fair chunk of change.

Location: Warehouse on the Call River
Time: 12 Wovoro, 989AF (Merge +35)

The warehouse was next to the Call River and about a mile downriver from Callbridge. It had doors big enough to load a river barge, but more importantly, it had a pasture next to it. There were sheep that grazed the pasture, but it was still a flat piece of ground that you could take an airplane off of.

Money from the stuff in the dwarven armory was going to pay for the rent for the next year. Freedric looked around with satisfaction.

They were finally getting started. Freedric, by now, had much of the design finalized. He was still working on the options for propulsion, but it would be a four seat aircraft, wings above the fuselage and tricycle landing gear.

Freedric and Alvin both knew how to fly, so once they got the thing built, they had people who could fly it.

He looked around the large building again, and in his mind, he laid out where the wings would be built and where the body would be assembled.

They hadn't the tools to build the tools yet. To make a wing, you needed struts and shaped wooden parts. To make those parts with anything like efficiency. You needed woodworking tools that went way beyond a file and a saw.

Location: Royce Townhouse, Callbridge
Time: 12 Wovoro, 989AF (Merge +35)

Alvin the Bard was at the moment very much Tim Walters. He was always the two of them, with the memories of both lives and a personality that fell somewhere between them. When he was onstage, he was more Alvin. In fact, most of the time he was more Alvin. Alvin was much better with people than Tim had ever been. But right now he wasn't on stage or dealing with people. He was designing the processes for making an electric motor. He wished that one of those chisels of stone shaping was a chisel of metal shaping instead. Alvin was a bard, shaping copper was rather out of his line. What he was trying to figure out was how much of the tools to build the tools could be replaced with magic.

Electricity was such a flexible product. Freedric was obsessed with his airplane, and that was fine. Nothing wrong with introducing aircraft to the world. But that was nothing compared to the advantages you would get from introducing electrical devices. Everything from boiling water to air conditioning. The Kingdom Isles were warmer than the British Isles of Tim Walters' world. They rarely froze even in winter, but electric heaters would still save lives.

Magic existed in this world, but it wasn't common. Even the magical knicknacks of Conley's Magic Shop were high end items that most people couldn't afford. Electricity and electrical devices . . . those could change the lives of millions of people around the world. They could introduce a middle class to a world that right now was mostly divided between peasants and lords.

To get interest in electronics, they needed to publicize its use and utility, and that brought Alvin right back to the airplane and an electric motor that would be efficient enough to be practical in the airplane.

That meant a hairpin engine but hairpin engines were put together by computer-control robots. Alvin went about the process of training a permanent servant amulet to act like a wire shaping robot.

Location: Warehouse on the Call River
Time: 14 Wovoro, 989AF (Merge +37)

Franklin Hunter looked at the drawing and wondered if Freedric the Incompetent was as incompetent as Conley said he was. He was also a bit worried that Freedric was paying him more than Conley had, but not enough more so that it was worth it if this company went bust and Franklin was left without a job. It wasn't exactly a teardrop shape that Freedric wanted. It was longer than that and flat on the bottom.

Well, he thought, *it's too late now. I already quit Conley's.* He took the awl and chisels and started carving the part that would be assembled to make the thing.

Freedric looked on as Franklin started carving the parts that would make up the ribs of the wing. Then he turned to his own work. Alvin had gotten Yahg involved in training the servants in the making of the electric motors that Alvin wanted to use to power the airplane. But Freedric wasn't convinced that electric motors were the way to go. There might be simpler, more straightforward, spells that would push the plane forward. Even just a stronger version of Alvin's lift spell might work. Get the plane high enough and it could glide for miles.

Maybe there was a spell that would act like a ramp. A ramp converted the downward force of gravity into forward motion. Of course, you had to be moving down for it to work. He went back to his magic books, looking for magical solutions.

Location: Royce Townhouse, Callbridge
Time: Evening, 14 Wovoro, 989AF

The servant placed the stewed beets and mutton on the table. They were eating solid, but not expensive fare, even if they were eating it off fine porcelain and using silver flatware.

"No, Freedric," Pip said. She was wearing dresses now. At least in the townhouse. Pip had dressed as a man for safety, not by preference. "Alvin's right. Even if you can make your magical ramp, even if you can make it so that the plane moves forward and not down, Alvin's still right. Because electricity is important. *More* important than airplanes. I want an electric air conditioner, heat pumps, and light bulbs, and radios, and telephones, computers, and blenders. I know that for ourselves with you and the books that Brian Royce had plus the books you found in the amulet safe, we can have all or at least most of those things through magic. But what about everyone else in the Kingdom Isles? Are you going to make enough magical items for all of them?"

"Are you going to make enough generators to power all those gadgets?" Freedric asked in turn.

"She doesn't need to, Freedric," Yahg said.

Freedric blinked in surprise. Yahg was about the most cold blooded man either Freedric or Jerry Garman had ever met. Not vicious unless he needed to be, but coldly willing to do what he saw as best for him and to hell with anyone in his way.

Yahg was still talking. "Once the use of electricity is understood even a little bit, and Alvin, with Tim's memories, understands it a lot better than that, the others will build the power plants and pay us for the privilege.

"So give up on other ways of doing it, at least for this first airplane. Concentrate on making a magical battery that will hold enough of a charge to power Alvin's motors for hours at a time. Something small and light that isn't part of the airplane, so that it won't need to be aged for too long to work."

Suddenly Freedric had it. A small and light battery. Shrink spells. If he could make a battery and shrink it while still being able to draw power from it, that would work. But there was a problem. Freedric remembered the *reduce item* spell from Jerry's memories and from Freedric's memories of the college of wizardry right here in Callbridge, but he didn't have it. It was a fifth level spell and not one that Freedric had ever had an opportunity to learn. Nor did he know if a shrunken battery would still work or would still hold the same charge. An ever full battery, like the ever full water cask that they'd found in the amulet safe would be better, but Freedric was pretty sure that such a device would need to be aged a decade at least to be of use.

He looked around the room and grinned. "You're all agreed?" he asked.

They nodded.

"Good enough. It will be an electric airplane with a magic battery," Freedric said.

* * *

An hour later, Freedric was in what had been Brian Royce's study, and by general agreement was now Freedric's, struggling through the Dwarven language textbooks. Dwarven wasn't Freedric's preferred language. He'd had to learn it in the wizard academy since so much magic was written in it, but he'd never liked it. At least the words were clear in the light of the crystals of light. Most light crystals put out the light of a candle. Not these. They'd been sitting in that amulet safe unactivated for centuries. A single light lit up the study like it was bright daylight shining through the roof.

Then he had it. Or maybe had it. If you have permanent sunlight, why not use a photocell? Could they make one that was efficient enough? Hell, could they make one at all? Freedric didn't know, but he knew that Alvin was going to have to get in touch with Tim Walters again.

Location: Royce Townhouse, Londinium
Time: Evening, 14 Wovoro, 989AF (Merge +37)

Albert Royce read the letter from his sister again. It read like her, but not like her. Debra had been a spoiled, entitled child as long as he'd known her.

He knew that people grew up.

People, yes.

But not Debra. At least he didn't think Debra would ever grow up. Could he be wrong? He didn't think so, but deep down he hoped so.

He was well off. Quite well off. He had estates in Derbyshire and business interests in Londinium and Normanland on the continent. He might send an agent, but that didn't seem right. To send a spy to investigate his family?

Sighing, he decided. He would go himself. It was an inconvenient trip. If he could go straight there, it would be eighty-two miles. But he couldn't go straight there. He was going to have to travel a hundred and thirty miles overland, or take a coaster almost four hundred miles around the island. Still, the packet boat would be both faster and more comfortable.

The next decision was whether he should take Emily. His daughter was eight and looking more like her mother every day. She would want to go. She would want to meet her uncles and aunt. But that wasn't going to happen. There was no way that Albert was going to expose his little girl to Brian, Charles, and Debra until he knew more about them. It might have been different if his wife Jane hadn't died. She could have handled them all. Albert was sure of that, but Emily was only eight. She would stay here in Londinium.

He set about making arrangements.

Location: Royce Townhouse
Time: Evening, 19 Wovoro, 989AF (Merge +42)

Alvin the Bard was trying to make a photocell. Because Alvin was a bard and Tim had never learned ancient languages, the dwarven books—for that matter, most of the Royce library—weren't all that valuable for this.

"What I need is an alchemist," he muttered. He knew from Tim's memories that there had been a lot of advances in the production of photocells. And he knew that the light put out by those dwarven light crystals had to be pretty intense right next to them. The trick was going to be to get a photo absorbent material that would convert the light into electricity. Assuming it really was light and not simply a magical illusion of light. That was the first thing he needed, a photometer. Then he needed to compare the light put out by the light crystals at various distances.

He got up and went to see if Freedric knew where he could find such a thing in this world.

Freedric didn't know, but he did know an alchemist. Fred Wilson owned a shop on Beaker Street. They headed for the front door. Charles and Debra were back in their maid and majordomo uniforms, because it turned out that Yahg was correct. They honestly didn't care about anything at all. They obeyed the instructions given, would answer questions, but didn't care about or want anything. They spent twelve hours each day in their cases to recharge, then they worked twelve hours, cleaning and maintaining the house, answering the door, then refusing entrance to anyone not authorized.

Freedric and Alvin were putting on their cloaks, preparing to leave the house, when the door knocker was struck.

Debra, dressed as a maid, went to the door and opened it.

There was a man there. He looked a bit like Brian Royce, save that he was older and thinner than Brian had been. He looked at Debra and said, "Sister, what are you doing dressed as a maid?"

"Oh crap," said Alvin. Freedric agreed with the sentiment, but Alvin, after a brief pause, said, "Debra, please invite your brother in. Freedric would you mind fetching Yahg, Pip, and Charles. And let Charles know that his brother, Albert, is here."

Freedric was pretty darn sure that the *sims* weren't going to fool Albert Royce for long. That, after all, was why Brian had moved to Callbridge. But he went. He suspected that they were going to need Yahg. On the other hand, he wasn't sure he could be a party to the murder of Albert Royce. The cold truth was Freedric didn't know what any of them could do.

* * *

Albert looked at his sister. She was not a day older than she had been ten years ago. She also looked calm, and that was wrong. Debra had been angry, often seductive, or at least trying to be, bubbly occasionally, but never calm. Also, the Debra he knew would never wear servant's garb. She would also never take instruction from anyone, much less someone that she would see as her social inferior. Which, from the way they were dressed, was both these fellows.

But she did. She stepped back and waved Albert in, saying, "Come in, Albert."

Albert followed her gesture into the front hall and looked around.

The fellow who'd told Debra to let him in was dressed in doublet and hose, with a cloak. Apparently the man had been preparing to leave. He was medium tall, perhaps five feet ten inches. He had brown wavy hair and green eyes in a tanned face with a friendly smile and even teeth. His clothing was worn, but well mended. He seemed to have been doing better in the last few weeks than in the preceding months. He was also acting like he owned the house that Albert's three siblings shared. He stepped forward, held out his right hand, and said, "Hello, Albert Royce. I'm Alvin the Bard."

Albert looked down at the man's hands and saw the calluses of a lute player's fingers. He also saw ink stains, the sort that adorned his own hands and those of anyone who worked regularly with quill and ink. Albert took the hand cautiously. "Hello, Alvin the Bard. What are you doing giving orders in the house rented by my siblings?"

"Oh, never orders, sir." Again that friendly, easy grin. "I am not the ordering sort. Advice is about as far as I go."

Albert had met this sort before. Sometimes they were honest, sometimes not, but they were always friendly and entertaining. It was their stock in trade, after all. "It sounded an awful lot like orders to me."

"Perhaps because the situation isn't what you were expecting," Alvin offered. "All will be explained, I imagine, but it will take a bit of time. It's been over ten years since you've seen any of your siblings and I didn't meet them until a few months ago. It's true that I am a guest in the house, but we are all involved in the business together, so . . ."

"So nothing, sir," Albert said. "My sister never would have taken advice from someone dressed as you are."

"That part had changed long before I got here, Mister Royce," Alvin said. "I fear I never knew the woman you describe."

About that time, Charles and . . . Great gods, that was an *orc* with him and the other fellow. Charles would spit on an orc sooner than speak with one. And Albert had often heard him say that they all ought to be killed.

The orc didn't seem to be hurrying particularly, but he was down the stairs quickly enough. Then Albert noticed the long handled battle axe, over the orc's shoulder and had a moment to be very thankful that he'd left his daughter back in Londinium, and to wonder if she was about to become an orphan. Then he saw a young woman in the sort of dress that his sister Debra used to love to wear come out onto the landing. In fact, Albert thought it might be one of Debra's dresses. She was short, five two or three, with short, sandy blonde hair, and blue eyes. She was thinner than Debra had ever been. But there was a smooth flow and litheness to her movement. She moved with a smooth, easy grace that surprised him and managed to make him forget about the axe bearing orc. At least long enough for the orc to move between Albert and the door.

Albert looked at the orc, then back at Alvin the Bard. "Just how much trouble am I in, sir?"

The orc gave a short, sharp laugh, and said, "That's going to depend on you."

The other fellow, Freedric, if Albert remembered correctly, said, "It's more a question of how much trouble we're *all* in. Us, as much as you. And we aren't really a party to any of it."

Albert had been looking at the young woman coming down the stairs when Freedric said that, and saw what looked to him like guilt flash across her face. He looked at Freedric and said, "I don't think the young lady agrees with you, sir."

"It's true about Freedric, Alvin, and Yahg," said the young woman and Albert was surprised to realize that he believed her.

The orc, presumably Yahg, said, "It wasn't your fault, either, Pip. You had no choice. I said so at the time."

Albert looked at him. He was still leaning against the front door, ax held loosely, but ready to attack if he decided to.

"Let's all go into the dining room and talk," said Alvin.

* * *

Alvin used *message* to ask Yahg,

"Tell him the truth?"

Yagh sent back.

Might as well, We won't get a lie past this one."

And that's what they did.

They had Charles tell most of it. The fact that Brian had killed them both and used the combined remittance of all of them to live like a lord. When he got to the part where Pip had woken him and had the key, so became the new master, Yahg took over and told of Brian, the explosion, and the rod of fireballs, and Pip using it on the cave cougars which killed him and Brian.

"So why aren't you dead?"

"Because of something called the Merge," Alvin said, and proceeded to explain about the Merge, the extra set of memories, each of them had gotten, and the curing of injuries.

* * *

It was a lot to take in. At the same time, what these people described was very much in character for his siblings. No one had ever been as real to Brian as his magical geegaws. His brother had murdered his other brother and his sister, and Albert had never known because Albert had never wanted to know.

He looked over at Pip.

She looked back, expecting censure and condemnation.

"Yahg was quite right, Miss," Albert said. "There was nothing else for you to do, given the circumstances. And, honestly—" Albert looked at the sim of his sister "—it was *less* than he deserved."

He looked around the table. "What I find less justified was your continuing to keep up the fraud, continuing to receive monies that my father's will promised to my *living* siblings."

"We haven't," said Alvin the Bard. "Your next payment to your siblings isn't due for another two months. If it fails to arrive, we will make no complaint."

"Of course not. What complaint could you make?" Albert snorted, "But what would you have done had I not visited? Would I have received a polite note informing me that Brian, Charles, and Debra no longer felt the need for the inheritance my father set aside for them? I somehow doubt it. And even less that I would have gotten word that my brothers and sisters had passed into Coganie's Hall that I might mourn them."

"Would you have mourned them?" Pip asked. "I've talked with Debra and Charles. I mean the *sims*, but they have all your brother and sister's memories of you, and they didn't think that you would care at all!"

Albert looked at her, and started to bluster, but under those eyes he just couldn't. "When they died, I probably wouldn't have," Albert admitted, "not until Jane, my wife, taught me to care for more than rules. But, yes, I do care now. I wish I could tell them that I am sorry for their loss and sorrier for my part in the estrangement between us."

The two *sims* sitting at the table with them didn't react to this profession of regret at all. They hadn't been told to simulate the responses of their models, so they didn't.

Albert wished they weren't here. They were like gravestones at the table. Reminders that his siblings were gone. That it was too late and past too late to correct the mistakes he'd made.

"All of which leaves us with the problem of what to do next," Yahg, the half-orc said.

Albert didn't cringe, but he was unfamiliar with and uncomfortable around orcs. Especially orcs who spoke decisively with excellent diction rather than in the slurred lower class speech of the south end. It wasn't what he was used to. At the same time, it did seem to endorse the truth of their claims of an extra set of memories.

"I don't know," he said, forcing himself to look the orc in the eyes. "You must know that whatever promises you force from me here in these rooms will not bind me once I am away. Your *sims* will have told you that while I am punctilious about my honor, I do not consider an oath given under threat binding."

He was surprised to see a grin on Yahg's face. "I like you, Albert. You've got balls. I'm going to regret having to kill you."

"We can't kill him, Yahg," said the little wizard. Freedric the Incompetent was five five and slight. He had black hair and black eyes in a brown face, and had ink stains on his fingers. He had the look of a book wizard or a clerk.

"Why ever not, Freedric? I know you're squeamish but . . ."

"Because killing him would involve Brian, Charles, and Debra inheriting, or at least being in a position to get control of his estates, until his daughter came of age. And that would involve an investigation by the Lord Mayor of Londinium, or his office. And that is the sort of investigation that would expose everything."

"So would him calling the constables as soon as he leaves," Yahg said. "Except we wouldn't have time to get away."

Pip looked around. "We aren't killing him, Yahg. Freedric and Alvin are opposed, and so am I. Three to one, and you agreed." Then she turned to Albert. "You have my word, Albert Royce, when we have finished our conversation, you will be free to leave."

Albert looked at her and felt a grin twitch his face. This young woman was clever. Since he had their assurance that he would be allowed to leave, any promises he made would be binding and if he should refuse to promise them his silence, she could change her mind. But as he looked at her, he didn't think she would.

"Very well. Now, how will you convince me not to proceed from your door to the residence of the Lord Mayor of Callbridge to demand that his office issue warrants for your arrest?"

"Arrest for what? Living in a house on which the rent is paid? Selling goods that we can make—" Alvin stopped, shook his head, and continued. "What would you gain? You have already acknowledged that we weren't at fault for the deaths of any of your siblings. There is nothing for you to revenge yourself on us for, and no profit to you in exposing us."

"And there may well be great profit to you in supporting us," Freedric said.

"What profit?" Albert asked. It was almost instinct and he felt like he was betraying his brothers and sister by asking such a question, only minutes after learning that all his siblings were dead.

That was when they told him about the airplane and the knowledge that they brought with them from those other people whose memories they had. Albert had always been good at finances. He was almost as focused on finances and management as Brian had been focused on magical items. It wasn't until Jane and, later, Emily, that he'd learned to care for others.

For the next several hours, they spoke of finances and business plans and he learned that Pip, with Betty Cartwright's memories, had an expertise in finances that he'd never seen before.

Albert's emotions were a swirling mass. Grief, anger, resentment, self-loathing, a profound desire to blame the messenger, to blame Yahg, Alvin, Freedric and Pip, even to blame the sims of his brother and sister for being there when his real brother and sister were in an unmarked grave. He knew that the desire to blame Yahg, Alvin, Freedric and Pip, was wrong. But he still felt it.

Worst of all was a small cowardly core of feeling that was grateful that he wouldn't have to deal with his siblings. That he could bury them, rather than face their resentment. The resentment that he had felt from them for as long as they had been in his life.

"I know how you feel," Pip said.

"You can't possibly know how I feel," Albert shot back.

"I have two children stolen from me by this Merge," Pip said. "I resent and am jealous of Betty Cartwright, and yet I know there is no justice in it. Betty is their real mother. I just remember being their mother. I wouldn't wish them here, in this world, and yet I do want them here in this world so that I might see them again. And I feel guilty for that wish. And I am Betty Cartwright as much as I am Pip. More in a way. I remember more than forty years of being Betty and not much more than twenty being Pip."

It wasn't the same, but yes, it was close enough that she probably did know something of how he felt. Feeling things that he knew it was wrong to feel. It helped in a strange way. It let him see Pip who was also Betty as a person like him, and through her, the rest of them, even Yahg.

* * *

By the time Albert left the townhouse the next day, he was convinced, and had given them his word freely that he wouldn't expose them, in exchange for which he was promised that when Charles and Debra officially died, their share in the business would come back to the family. That, with the share he was buying, would give Albert a three-seventh share of the company.

Albert's emotions were still a confused mass, but Albert had always been able to put emotions aside and consider things logically when he needed to. It was one of the things that his younger siblings had resented most about him.

Albert would also be investing enough to put the company on a sound financial footing.

Location: Royce Townhouse
Time: Evening, 21 Wovoro, 989AF

As Albert entered the dining room, Yahg and Pip were arguing about something that made no sense. "Edward's based on Henry V," Yahg was saying, but Pip was shaking her head.

"No." She held up a hand. "I don't mean that they didn't base him on Henry, but none of those guys studied enough actual history to make the analogy hold up."

"Pull up a chair, Albert," said Alvin the Bard. "The show just started. You haven't missed much."

Pip made a rude gesture and Albert had to work hard not to laugh.

He moved over to Alvin and took a seat. "What is the play about?"

He waved at Yahg and Pip. Pip, who he was coming to think of as Betty Cartwright.

Alvin leaned his head to whisper, "They are still debating how much influence the history of our player's world had on the design of ours." Then in a louder voice, he said, "You should ask Albert. He operates in the halls of the mighty."

"That's an excellent idea," Betty said. "What is the situation in Parise."

"Why do you want to know?" Albert asked. He was involved in the government, but that meant that he had to be careful of what he said to anyone.

"We're trying to determine to what extent the conflict between the Kingdom Isles and Parise is analogous to the Hundred Years War between England and France."

"Hundred Years War?" Albert asked. The war with Parise was already costing the crown a great deal and King Arthur III wasn't happy with the cost.

"Yes. In the . . ." For the next fifteen minutes Yahg lectured them all on the Hundred Years War and the many WarSpell scenarios that copied parts of it. How Edward III of England was analogous to Boudicca IV and the Parise law about male secession. "Which they got from the dwarves. A most patriarchal people," Yahg added.

The Pendragon line in The Kingdom Isles had always included women in the line of succession. The heir was the eldest child of the present monarch without regard to gender if the present monarch died without naming a successor. If there were no children, as was the case with "the last legitimate King of Parise," then it went to the closest blood tie without regard to gender. By Kingdom law anyway. By Parisian law passed after the last legitimate king died, it went to the closest male line.

"Queen Boudicca IV was willing to let it pass to Arthur," Albert said, "but the Parisians insisted that she couldn't give her son what she didn't have. What it amounted to was that the lords of Parise didn't want to bend the knee to an 'Islander barbarian.' "

"Okay fine," Yahg said. "The initial negotiations broke down in 915 and Boudicca IV had taken Normandland from Parise and made several other gains. Then she died in 975 and King Arthur III agreed to a peace in place, which the Parisians started chipping away at until two years ago when they determined that Normanland was part of Parise and could not be ruled by a foreign prince."

"Which was when Edward insisted that they had to take up arms. Arthur had no love for war, and not much for the Normanlands, save as a source of taxes, but to let the Pariseians get away with their seizure of the Normanlands would cause the Kingdom to be permanently relegated to a third rate power." Albert was quite incensed by that idea.

Betty looked at him. She was rather less incensed. Betty was born and raised in a republic and saw the actions of kings as next to criminal. But she liked Albert's loyalty.

"The point is," Yahg continued, "this time in the game worlds is roughly, very roughly, analogous to the 13th century in our history." He waved at the other merged people at the table. "There are several scenarios that cover the Battle of Agincourt which, from what I understand, won't be happening in this timeline since the dauphin got sick and won't lead the chivalry of France into a trap." Then he stopped and looked at Albert for so long that Albert started to think that he was reconsidering leaving Albert alive.

Then Yahg looked at Betty and sighed. "Albert, what we are trying to decide is if the Kingdom Isles can become the second cradle of democracy that, to an extent, England did in our timeline. And if we should help it or try to tear it down. Understand, the world we come from would be analogous to your world somewhere around the year 1700 or 1800. Things like Alvin's electricity and Freedric's airplane are the least of it. Our world was a world of freedom and individual rights. Rights shared not just by the nobles and knights, but by every citizen in the land from richest to poorest. That means an orc like me has exactly the same rights as you. Can the Kingdom Isles become a place where that is true?"

Albert had suffered several shocks to his system over the last few days. He'd talked to Yahg and found him to be among the smartest people he'd ever met. Smarter even than Freedric, and everyone knew that wizards were incredibly intelligent. He looked at Betty, the young yet mature woman who was increasingly finding a place in his heart, and knew that, absent intervention, she like Yahg would never have the rights of a man or woman of the nobility or gentry.

He looked back at Yahg. "I think it's worth the effort to try."

CHAPTER 7: A CHANGE IN STATUS

Location: Lord Mayor's Office, Callbridge
Time: Mid-morning, 23 Wovoro, 989AF

The clerk looked up as the two women and the orc entered the office. The orc was clearly a bodyguard, but he still almost ordered him out. Would have, except that he was carrying a battle ax that had a blade that was clearly of dwarvish make. Which meant that the two young women were rich.

Between the two women and the orc, it was almost half a minute before the man with them registered with the clerk. Not until he stepped around the women and announced, "I am Albert Royce of Londinium. I'm here to register with the office of the Lord Mayor, the unfortunate demise of my brother, Brian, late of this town. And to inform the Lord Mayor's office that the family will be taking on any *provable* debts he had outstanding at his death."

That was less of a surprise than it might have been. Brian Royce had been a show-off, accustomed to having dinners and spending lavishly until the last few weeks, during which he was rumored to be ill or injured. "Very well, sir. Are these ladies with you?"

"Yes. This is Debra Royce, Brian's younger sister. With the assistance of Betty Cartwright—" He waved at the other young woman. "—she will be handling all of the finances for now. Our brother, Charles, will have other responsibilities, so will be unable to assist."

The clerk wasn't happy about this. This was the Kingdom Isles, not Parise, so women could inherit property and titles. Even so, women didn't usually conduct business in Callbridge.

Still, between the Londinium connection and the orc with the battle axe, he didn't argue.

Location: Royce Townhouse, Callbridge
Time: Mid-afternoon, 24 Wovoro, 989AF

"I've been away too long," Albert Royce said, looking at Pip, aka Betty Cartwright, utterly ignoring the two sims. And not paying much more attention to the men in the room.

"I hope you will be able to return soon," Pip answered. "I will write, telling you how things are going here."

Albert nodded, then took her hand and kissed it, then turned and left.

* * *

The guys didn't say "woo hoo," but the looks they gave each other were almost more irritating. Pip could still feel the brush of Albert's lips across the back of her hand. Pip had learned early that sex was a painful business, best to be avoided at all cost. But Betty Cartwright had had a full, rich and healthy sexlife. And those experiences had gone a long way to fixing the issues that Pip's life had given her. She was ready for a bit of romance in her life. Ready to be a woman, if there was the right man in the picture.

She was coming to believe that Albert Royce was that right man.

Albert had taken with him most of the rest of the goods from the Dwarven tunnels, and in exchange had left enough money to pay off the rest of Brian's debts and enough of a drawing account to allow them to introduce mimeograph printing.

It would be a bit slower than the Z-rocks magical item, but once you had a sheet you could make hundreds of copies, not one or two.

Location: Royce Townhouse, Callbridge
Time: Mid-afternoon, 2 Estormany, 989AF

It was finished. The mimeograph was done and ready to print. They'd even printed several test pages and they had a five page pamphlet on the purification of water by use of a charcoal filter. It was mostly drawings with just a bit of text. They started hand cranking the mimeograph and two hours later, after five stencil changes, they had five hundred copies of the pamphlet. Freedric took a dozen copies to the library at Callbridge University and offered fifty of them on consignment to a bookseller he knew. The rest were packaged up and sent to Albert in Londinium

* * *

Over the next couple of weeks, they were approached by dozens of scholars from the university at Callbridge about printing their tracts on this, that, and everything else. When offered adequate payment, they did so.

Meanwhile, at the shop where the airplane was under construction, they had produced an example of a Coleman lantern. It still had problems, but it worked. It, too, was sent to Albert in Londinium.

Location: Royce Townhouse, Londinium
Time: Mid-afternoon, 10 Estormany, 989AF

Albert Royce was a knight, responsible to his liege lord, and that liege lord arrived on his doorstep three days after he had sent the new "Royce lantern" off to the smith to be reproduced and put into production.

"By the gods, Albert," Lord Tenhoks demanded as soon as his cloak was off his shoulders, "how did you come up with that lantern thingamabob? It works like magic, but my wizard insists that there's nothing magical about it."

"He's quite right, Your Grace," Albert said, standing and waving His Grace to a chair. His Grace, the Duke of the South March of Wiles, was a friend of King Arthur III and of his son Edward the prince and heir, who was off in Parise, fighting a siege on the Centriaum coast.

Albert was here in the Kingdom Isles because Arthur III felt he was of more use as an income source than as a soldier in the field. Arthur III was right. Albert was competent with a sword, but only competent. He was, like his father before him, skilled at managing estates and making money. In fact, both the king and His Grace owed him a fair amount. "The lamp is the product of research and creative thinking."

"Of your brother, Brian?" the duke asked as he took the offered chair and waved impatiently for Albert to sit back down.

"No, Your Grace," Albert sat, remembering Brian's murder of Charles and Debra. "Brian never created much of anything!"

"Very well, Albert. We'll leave off discussion of your brother. If his death hasn't healed the breach between you, I doubt anything will." There was a note of censure in the duke's voice.

"I'm sorry, Your Grace, but I learned things about my brother and his life that I would rather not have known."

"Then where did these lamps come from?"

"They were invented by Freedric the Wizard, Betty Cartwright, and Alvin the Bard." Albert concluded that mentioning Yahg, the half-orc, was probably not going to be helpful. For, in discussions with Yahg and Betty, Albert had come to the conclusion that if the rights of His Majesty's subjects were to be expanded, it would be through the king, not the nobles. Nobles who would likely see increasing the rights of commoners as decreasing their rights.

"Who the heck are Freedric—" The duke waved his hands vaguely. "—those people."

"Adventurers who have proven to have hidden depths," Albert said. Explaining the double sets of memories wasn't something that Albert wanted to try, which meant he needed a better explanation. He wasn't nearly so facile as Alvin the Bard, but he did know his audience. The duke didn't actually care where the lamps came from. What he cared about was how much profit they would bring and making sure that he would get a share of it. By preference, the lion's share. "Your Grace, Freedric the Wizard is an inventor of devices. The lamps and the drum stencil printers are just the first."

"What are drum stencil printers?"

"A means of making many copies of a document cheaply."

The duke didn't read. He was an intelligent man and did know how to read, but he didn't enjoy it and books were horribly expensive, so the duke had people to do the reading of accounts for him, and for the rest he had storytellers and bards.

"Those pamphlets on the purification of water by use of a charcoal filter? My wizard Conroy was blathering about those. Also from your group of adventurers?"

"Yes, Your Grace," Albert said. "And another thing they know how to do is go to ground, should they feel the need."

The duke gave him a sharp look. "Delicate handling?"

"Kid gloves, Your Grace, from start to finish. And the finish, if we live to see it, will be decades hence."

His Grace leaned back in the chair and examined Albert. Examined him so long that Albert was getting nervous. "Very well, Albert. I have trusted you in matters of management and you have proved very good at it. But right now, I want to know how much you think these adventurers are going to be worth to crown and country."

Albert considered. He'd been considering since before he'd left the townhouse in Callbridge. When he wasn't thinking about Pip, that is. Freedric and Alvin were smart in their way, but it was a focused sort of intelligence, the sort that was good at doing one thing, not figuring out the consequences. Yahg and Pip were more rounded. Apparently John Kipler had been a reader of everything that he could find in a world that was full of books. He'd read history, sciences, philosophy, and he'd read extensively on the game of WarSpell and the settings it took place in. He knew the military situation in Parise better than Albert had. It was Yahg and Pip's assessment that Albert was guided by. Pip or rather Betty Cartright read as extensively as John Kipler and if her reading was more fiction oriented it was very valuable. The "industrial revolution" that Yahg and Pip talked about and fractional reserve banking and full faith and credit money that Pip had discussed all meant a major change in the world.

Albert swallowed. "By the time my daughter's children are grown, Your Grace, more than all the gold in the Kingdom Isles."

The duke laughed, then stopped laughing. "You really believe that, don't you?"

Albert nodded solemnly.

Again the duke looked at him for a very long time. "I will be seeing His Majesty at the end of the week. I'll be discussing this with him. Who else should I discuss it with?"

"For now, no one, Your Grace. But in a few months, I will need to have some long discussions with the royal exchequer and several of the lords of parliament."

His Grace left soon after, and Albert went back to thinking about Pip.

Location: Royce Townhouse, Callbridge
Time: Mid-afternoon, 12 Estormany, 989AF

Pip passed a hand over the silk gown that she had inherited from Debra Royce. It was ten years out of style in Londinium, but it was the nicest dress Pip had ever owned. Then she forcefully took her mind off the dress, how she looked in it, and how Albert Royce might look at her as she wore it. She, with effort, put that all aside and focused on everything she remembered about the introduction of paper money. It wasn't much.

She would talk to Yahg and she would talk to Alvin. Alvin wouldn't know, but he could ask Tim Walters. Tim wouldn't know either, but he had access to Merge World libraries. The problem with that, was that getting those libraries one sentence at a time wasn't a workable solution, even if the spell wasn't one that would exhaust, even kill, Alvin if it was cast too often. But she could ask what the one thing that she most needed to know about paper money was, and hope there was only one thing.

She got up, took her notes, and went to talk to Yahg. Yahg wasn't in the townhouse.

Location: Mortemer's Tavern and Trinkets
Time: Mid-afternoon, 12 Estormany, 989AF

Alvin the Bard looked over at Yahg. Yahg's family hadn't come up in game play. Alvin had known that Yahg had a family, just as Alvin did, but Alvin was out of touch with his family.

Yahg wasn't. He had a mother and a father. His mother was human, and his father was a bone collector. Basically, a garbage man, who made his living by collecting and sorting trash to sell it to the businesses that used it. His father hadn't approved of Yahg's choice of occupation, because he didn't want his son getting killed.

Yahg had taken up his occupation mostly to protect his family from the guild. As a member, he was in a position to mark them as off limits. But that protection was disappearing as Yahg stepped away from the guild. He also had a younger brother and a sister, both of them smarter than Yahg had been before the Merge. And, in Yahg's opinion, both of them were in need of an education. Which Alvin and Freedric could provide in the form of employment. But first it would have to be cleared with the guild.

Alvin knocked on the door. The peephole in the door opened. Yahg put his face in front of it, and said, "Open it." He gave no password. Yahg almost never did.

The door opened. Alvin asked, "Think that would work for me?"

Yahg grunted, keeping in character.

"No," said the door guard. "It wouldn't."

"We're here for a couple of things," Alvin said. "To pay off the last of Pip's buyout, and to arrange things so that the guild will continue to leave Yahg's family alone."

"How you figure on doing that?" asked the door guard with a sneer.

Yahg didn't say a word. He did turn like a cat, and shove a gauntleted fist into the belly of the door guard. As the man bent double, Yahg reached out, grabbed him by the neck, lifted him up, and slammed him into the wall. By the time the man hit the floor, there were knives, swords, and cudgels, as well as a couple of axes, out and people were starting to rise from their benches.

"That could happen to the guild entire," Alvin said in a loud, but friendly, voice, as he pointed at the door guard on the floor. "And if you folks don't settle down, it will."

"Oh, and how's that?" Maggs asked. "You going to call in the King's Own?"

The King's Own were an elite unit. They were all belted knights, and they were tough. Everyone knew that.

"I won't," Alvin said, "but Albert Royce will."

"Never heard of him," Mack the Cudgel said.

"Then you should pay attention," said Pete the Cat. "He was here last month, when we learned that Brian Royce was dead. He lives in Londinium and has the ear of the duke of the South March. Who, as I'm sure you don't know, is a close friend of His Majesty." He looked around the room and then made patting motions with both hands. "Everyone settle down. Alvin, you and Yahg come over here and let's talk."

As people regained their seats, Alvin and Yahg walked to the corner table where the ruling council of the guild of thieves sat.

Alvin sat, but Yahg didn't. The big orc stood behind the bench Alvin was sitting on, and glared angrily around the room. Yahg was now smarter than most anyone in the room. He was bright enough to keep silent about his intelligence, but that didn't make it easy. He looked around the room, trying not to be obvious. The floor was earth with straw laid out on it, then compressed by people walking on it. Every month or so, they would shovel out the crushed straw and lay down another batch. The straw absorbed the stuff that got dropped on the floor, and after it was crushed it was a decent fertilizer. The wood furniture was not well made. It was all as familiar to him as his boots.

Yet, looked at through John Kipler's memories, it was a spaghetti western on steroids. There was no magic here. Nothing of wealth or prominence, and damn little of beauty. Yahg almost shook his head. *This* was the sort of life that John Kipler had aspired to? John Kipler had been a bright and bitter man who escaped into books and RPGs because of his physical weakness. A man who had never had any physical prowess and almost no friends.

Alvin was speaking quietly to the four members of the council. A new fifth member had still not been appointed. The death of the thugs who attacked them had been a hammer blow to the internal politics of the guild. It was threatening to put the cut purses in ascendance again.

Yahg didn't give a crap. As long as they left him and his family alone, the guild could do whatever it wanted.

Tommy the Black was saying, "Where's our cut of these new toys?"

Yahg bent, planted his hands on the table, and brought his face to within inches of Tommy the Black's. "You want a cut? I cut your head off. You like that cut?"

"Again, though my large friend is putting it poorly, attempting to extort us will produce bad results. The king and the exchequer have an interest in what we are doing. Any accidents that happen to our shops or us will bring retribution." Alvin pressed the air above the table in a soothing petting gesture. "It's always been the policy of the guild to avoid offending anyone of the nobility. The profit isn't worth the cost. Yahg and his family, as well as myself, Pip, Freedric, Debra and Charles Royce should be moved into that category. It's the best thing for the guild, it really is."

"A frigging orc in the nobility?" demanded Mack the Cudgel. "The Kingdom Isles will sink into the sea before that happens."

Almost, Yahg killed Mack then. Almost. A rage that was half Yahg's and half John Kipler's welled up in him and he was restrained as much by habit of acceptance as by Kipler's understanding that it would be a suicide move, not just for him, but for his whole family. For the word "orc" in the Kingdom Isles had all the same connotations of the "N" word in John's world.

Somehow he kept himself from acting, but something in his face must have shone through. Mack visibly paled.

"Relax, Yahg," Alvin said, and Yahg wanted to hit him. But Alvin was on his side. He just didn't understand because he'd never been an orc in the Kingdom Isles.

They made their case and got out.

* * *

On the walk back, Alvin said, "You almost gave yourself away back there, Yahg. I know you're smarter than me. Tim was a bright guy, but focused on electrical engineering to the exception of just about everything else. Your education has been a lot broader, but you looked like you were ready to lose it back there. What happened?"

"I'm not sure," Yahg said. "Twenty-five years of swallowed rage. Rage swallowed by habit. Forced down by the fact that everyone, even my father, basically agrees with Tommy the Black. That *I* agreed with Tommy in some deep recess of my soul. Right up until I got John's memories. Orcs are slavering monsters. Everyone knows it, even the orcs."

Suddenly Alvin stopped in the middle of the cobble stone street and asked, "Where the hell did the orcs come from? I mean we don't have any ships traveling to the Orclands, or the Elflands, for that matter. But there are orc tribes on the Kingdom Isles and occasional elves are seen."

The totally geeked out Tim Walters question brought Yahg back to himself. He laughed a deep, echoing laugh that bounced off the walls of the buildings on either side of the street. "I guess you never read the origin story."

"No. I didn't play but that single game, and I guess Alvin never knew."

"At the height of the Dwarven Empire, they started experimenting with magical doorways that went from one place to another. The idea was to let the clans of the central mountain ranges move their forces from the central mountains to the outlying provinces, even the Kingdom Isles. But their guidance didn't work all that well. They opened up a gate from one underground tunnel to another, but not necessarily the one they were after. They ended up with tunnels that went to caves in the Orclands and the Elflands. At first it looked like a good thing. New worlds to conquer, and all that. But the orcs were tough and the elves subtle and neither group was all that fond of the invading dwarves, so there were counter attacks. After about two hundred years of back and forth, there were small colonies of orcs and very small colonies of elves on Centraium and in the Kingdom Isles. Lizard men, too.

"They managed to shut most of the gates down and the whole thing was given up as a bad job. The orcs and elves were almost eradicated. But small tribes were left. The magic of the gates is screwy too. The gates will open up now and again, dumping a couple of hundred orcs into the Kingdom. They mostly get killed or made into slaves. Sometimes they will escape into abandoned Dwarven tunnels. Unless they get out of hand, the nobles don't bother digging them out."

"Anyway, my family, well, my father's family, arrived in the Isles through one of those doors."

"Magic," Alvin said, "is a pain in the arse."

"It's not magic. It's people. We want to be on top so we want someone else to be on the bottom."

CHAPTER 8: BUILDING THE TOOLS

Location: Royce Townhouse, Callbridge
Time: Mid-afternoon, 15 Cashi, 989AF

Fred Wilson, a prominent alchemist from Londinium, placed the black quartz crystal on the table between them. Alvin looked at it. It was a beautiful thing, shiny black, but it wasn't what he was after. He was after black silicon, which made the most efficient photocells.

"Sorry, Fred. It's beautiful, but it's not what we need."

Fred was arguing with him about the nature of matter. They were working together on trying to develop a substance that would absorb light and make electricity, which was still the stumbling block on making a practical airplane.

The airframe was finished. So was the electric motor that would push it through the air. After a lot of back and forth, they'd gone with a pusher motor above the main body of the airplane.

In the meantime, they'd introduced the propeller, the steam turbine, and over fifty other devices. Fred had been quite helpful in letting Alvin and Freedric develop a battery that could be recharged by a spell. The problem was the battery was heavy and not that strong. It weighed over a hundred pounds and it would run the electric motor for about ten minutes before running out of power.

The steam turbines were busily pumping out tin mines in northern Wiles and the price of tin had dropped by almost ten percent.

Albert Royce and his allies at the king's court in Londinium were happy, but there were rumblings of discontent.

The gadgets were going first to Albert and his friends at court. The other factions at court didn't like that, according to Albert's latest letter to Pip anyway. The innovations they had introduced weren't yet having all that much of an effect on the economy. The economy of the Kingdom Isles was way too large to be seriously affected by a few mimeograph machines and steam saws. It would be years before the effects of increasing productivity would be felt nationwide.

Locally it was a different story. They were in an extended truce with the thieves guild and Yahg's younger brother and sister had jobs at the airplane shop. They had also hired Marcy Louise Caris, who was an intercessor of Prima, learning about disinfectants. Marcy didn't get spells from Prima. Most intercessors didn't, no matter what god they followed.

Alvin was getting worried. Tim had never been all that interested in how money worked, so Alvin's knowledge of economics was almost non-existent. But Callbridge was suffering inflation. It was localized but the cost of eggs, bacon, wheat, and rye had all gone up.

According to Pip, aka Betty, that was because of them. They were taking the money Albert was sending them for the inventions and spending it hiring people, including Yahg's whole family, as well as a lot of others of the poor of Callbridge. Those people spent their wages on eggs and butter, on clothing, and better rooms and so on, and the local farmers were having more customers and were charging more.

Alvin shook his head at the worrying distraction, and went back to work on the photocell.

* * *

In another room of the townhouse, Freedric was struggling through the dwarven magic books. They were useful in a way, but at the same time Freedric was increasingly convinced that at least half the problems he was facing was the fact that the books were full of assumptions about magic and how it flowed that were just wrong.

There was a knock and he looked up to see Pip at the door.

"The cloth merchant wants five coppers a yard for basic weave wool."

Freedric blinked. "Is that a lot?"

"Yes, Freedric, that's a lot," Pip said. "I've been working up a market basket."

Freedric blinked again, then remembered. The market baskets were from back on Earth, what they were now calling the Merge world. They were a way of determining the value of money. "So what do you want me to do about it?"

"I don't know, but we're introducing a lot of products into the Kingdom's money supply. In exchange, we're getting a lot of money which we're spending locally, meaning that prices are going up here. But money is getting scarce somewhere else. I don't know where, but I'm guessing it's either in Londinium or in the countryside."

"Some of that money is coming from Centraium," Freedric said. "Albert says that they are selling a lot of tin in Dorchry."

"Mercantilism," Pip said.

"Okay, Pip. What is mercantilism?"

"It's the economic theory that is based on the belief that the road to national wealth is through selling more to other countries and buying less."

"Makes sense to me," Freedric said.

"Yes, I know. It makes sense to me too, but I know from Betty's econ 101 class that it's wrong, primitive, and generally a bad idea. What I don't know, or can't remember, is why."

Freedric scratched his chin. He didn't know crap about economics and didn't care. Or at least he hadn't cared about economics back on Earth. Or here, for that matter, before the Merge. "Aren't the gods supposed to know about this stuff?"

"Right. I can just see myself going to the temple of Cashi and asking about the market basket."

"That might not be a bad idea," Freedric started, then patted the air when it looked like Pip was going to interrupt. "No, hear me out. There are recall spells that let you remember stuff clearly. Couldn't you get an intercessor to cast one on you to remember your econ classes?"

"Maybe. Would that give the gods access to our memories? I don't want the intercessors of Cashi deciding that I am possessed."

"I guess it depends on how important it is that you remember what you know."

Location: Royce Townhouse, Londinium
Time: Mid-afternoon, 19 Cashi, 989AF

Pip climbed down from the carriage, followed by Yahg. He was, as usual, acting his role as sullen and stupid retainer, and by now Pip was getting worried. It was eating at him in a way it hadn't before the Merge.

The door to the Royce townhouse in Londinium opened and Albert came out. He first went to Yahg and stuck out his hand, just as though Yahg was a belted knight. Pip was shocked and just a bit annoyed that Albert would greet Yahg first.

Yahg was looking shocked. Then, as the hand stayed out and Albert looked him in the eye, he started to smile. He reached out and took the offered hand in his. And they shook. Right there on the street, in front of the servants, the neighbors. and the gods. "Welcome to my home," Albert said. Then he turned to Pip.

Again he held out his hand, but when she put hers in it, he lifted it to his lips and kissed it. "It's good to see you, Betty."

He turned to his servants and said, "Take our guests' bags. Put Yahg in the second floor guest room and Betty in the third. And inform Cook that there will be two more for dinner."

* * *

A few minutes later, after Pip and Yahg had been introduced to Albert's daughter, they settled into seats in Albert's study. There were some obvious changes. There were filing cabinets along one wall. They were clearly new and built to designs that Freedric had sent a couple of weeks ago. They were oak stained dark brown and polished to a high gloss.

"I'm glad to see you. Alvin warned me that you were coming, but didn't say much about why you were coming?"

"Pip's worried about the economy," Yahg said.

"I can speak for myself," Pip said, lightly rubbing her hand where Albert had kissed it. "He's right, though. Betty was a bank teller, not an economics professor. She'd taken some economics, enough to have a handle on what the jargon meant, but not enough to really understand how it all worked. Much less how it works in this world."

"So what has you worried?"

"That's harder to explain. Inflation, stagflation, deflation. I know that a bunch of experts spent a lot of time and a lot of money trying to make sure that there was enough product to match the money and enough money to match the economy. Fractional reserve banking as a way of introducing money without debasing currency and what's dangerous about it. I just can't remember enough. Freedric suggested that perhaps a spell of remembrance would let me remember more. And while John had less formal education in economics than Betty did, I think that Yahg might remember even more."

"Such spells are expensive."

This was a low magic world, with the average wizard somewhere around seventh level. A bit more than Freedric, but not the twentieth-level wizards that some game worlds boasted.

"Which god?"

The present patron god of the Kingdom Isles was Wovoro, the god of the seas, but increasingly the goddess Cashi was popular in the coffee houses near the warehouses of Londinium. There were other gods but those two had the largest presence in the Kingdom Isles.

"How confident are you that they really are getting spells?" Yahg asked.

"We know some do. There are the occasional healings and some of the spells Wovoro has given intercessors have saved ships. Cashi seems pretty anxious to weed out frauds. She has a geas that she has her intercessors place on hucksters that forces them to speak only truth. I'm told that it's unpleasant, even if you're a basically honest person. What I'm concerned with is you, either of you, giving access to your minds to Cashi, Wovoro, or any of the rest."

"Me too," Pip acknowledged.

* * *

Later at dinner Pip, Albert, his daughter Emily, and Yahg spoke of airplanes and steam engines, and Pip showed off her sleight of hand by making a copper coin appear out of Emily's ear. All while the servants looked on.

"No, it's an issue of laminar flow," Yahg was saying as a servant placed a bowl of soup before him. "Thank you," he said to the servant, then turned back to Albert. "The more the laminar flow is disrupted, the greater the parasitic drag. That slows the aircraft and that decreases the lift. That's why everything has to be smooth."

* * *

In the kitchen of the townhouse, the cook listened in disbelief as Margret insisted that Yahg had to be the smartest orc in creation. "They were talking about some sort of laminier and how it flowed."

"What's laminier?"

Margret shrugged. "I don't know. Maybe something in the air, but it invites parasites which hook on the wings of the arieo-planes and try to drag them back to the ground."

The cook wasn't buying. Orcs were stupid. Everyone knew that. Strong and vicious, powerful fighters, especially in caves and other places underground, but stupid.

It didn't matter. Margret was a talkative woman and she repeated the story. So did the other servants who had listened to the master and his guests talking. Albert Royce was an important man. Not a personal confidant of the king, but a confidant of a couple of the king's counselors. The servants also knew from other guests that Albert's star was rising. Which only added to the rumors.

Location: Temple of Cashi, Londinium
Time: Mid-afternoon, 21 Cashi, 989AF

High Intercessor of Cashi Michael J. Lowrey did receive spells. Not a lot, but he received them. It had been of great help in his ascendance through the hierarchy of the temple. But the real reason that he was the High Intercessor for all the Kingdom Isles was that he had a phenomenal memory and kept excellent track of who was who in the political world of the kingdom.

He stood and bowed slightly as Albert Royce came in, followed by a young woman and a large, well armed orc.

As a rule Michael wasn't overly fond of orcs. Cashi was the goddess of trading, not raiding, and orcs, at least by reputation, were much too fond of stealing for his taste. He was also very curious because according to the rapidly spreading rumor, the orc had to be Yahg, the "smartest orc in the world."

"Welcome, Sir Royce," he said. "Will you introduce your companions?"

"These are Betty Cartwright and Yahg Fortonson," Albert said, waving at each in turn. "We are here to discuss the cost of a spell of remembrance. Two spells of remembrance." Neither Pip nor Yahg actually had a last name. In Pip's case they'd decided to use Betty Cartwright the name of her merge. Yagh though had a family, if not a legally recognized one. So in Yahg's case they based the family name on Yahg's father's name. Hence forth, they would all be Fortonsons. Yahg, his brother Paul, and sister Elizabeth, even his parents.

"According to rumor, Yahg here is the smartest orc in the world. What does he need help in remembering?"

The orc blinked. He was clearly surprised, but Michael wasn't sure if he was pleased or upset. Then Michael remembered something else. When the woman and the orc had arrived, Albert had greeted the orc as an equal in public. He stretched out a hand to Yahg. "What is it you want to remember, Yahg Fortonson?"

After another look of surprise, Yahg took his hand and then gave a little half smile and answered. "How to introduce great wealth into an economy without damaging it beyond repair."

Michael Lowrey looked at the orc in complete shock because Michael was probably as much of an expert on how economies worked as this world had, which meant he knew enough to realize that it wasn't a stupid question.

He looked over at Albert Royce who was looking at Yahg in irritated surprise. An expression that was hidden as soon as Albert saw him looking. "I take it I wasn't to have that explained to me?"

"Well, it is a rather private matter."

Michael's office had a desk behind which was a high chair. There was also a couch and a low table. Michael waved them to the couch. Albert sat next to Betty and Michael sat next to Yahg, having utterly forgotten that the man was an orc.

"Tell me what this is all about, please. If what Yahg Fortonson said is accurate, I think the temple of Cashi will be buying or at least attempting to buy whatever he and Miss Cartwright remember for rather more than the spells would cost."

* * *

Yahg looked around the room. What these folks called a desk was what would be called a lectern back on Earth. The room was white washed and there were coins of light in each corner, and another placed right over the desk/lectern where Yahg imagined Michael J. Lowrey did most of his work. He was a solidly built man with a beard and hair that was reddish brown.

And he'd greeted Yahg like he was a person, not a guard dog or dangerous predator. That was what had decided Yahg to trust the man. It was a shock. And as he thought about it, it told Yahg quite a lot about the High Intercessor of Cashi. This man was smart and his intellect took precedence over any emotions he might have.

"I want to remember a course of study I took on the subject of economics and Pip, officially Betty Cartwright, wants to remember the same thing. We also want anything we can remember about Keynes, Friedman, and Greenspan." He felt himself smile. "Also Adam Smith and Karl Marx."

That brought a laugh from Pip. Then at Lowrey's look, she said, "It's just the thought of Yahg wanting to remember the father of communism's words of wisdom."

"Well, if this Adam Smith has any wisdom to share, I would like to hear them, whatever communism is."

Pip laughed again.

"In any case," Lowrey continued, "I am an expert on money and how it works. At least, I like to think I am. I've read all the scholars on the subject and I have never heard of Marx, Greenspan, Friedman or any of the rest, so who are they and how do you know about them? I'm not prying without reason. It will help in my prayers to Cashi if I know the specifics."

Yahg looked at Pip, who looked back, then shrugged, tacitly leaving it to Yahg to decide.

"If I tell you this, what assurance do I have it will go no further?"

"All the temples of all the gods have the rite of the confessional. And we are all obligated by our gods to keep what is said private. Assuming it's not an offense against our gods. Sometimes even if it is."

And Yahg could believe as much of that as he chose. "On the fifth of Pago, Pip and I were exploring in dwarven tunnels when we were both killed or almost killed. In the moment of our not quite deaths, something strange happened. Each of us acquired the memories and knowledge of another person. I got the memories of John Kipler and Pip got the memories of Betty Cartwright. Both Betty and John were reasonably well educated in a world that was full of books and knowledge. Some of those books, some of that knowledge, has to do with how to make things. Other parts of it has to do with the way money works and how to introduce money into the world so that it will match a world of increasing wealth."

"Are you still yourselves?" There was real concern in Lowrey's voice.

Yahg shrugged. "Are you still the person who you were ten years ago?"

"No, I'm not, but I *am* still Michael Lowrey."

"I still remember everything I remembered as Yahg. So, like you, I'm not still the same person I was before the Merge, but I *am* still Yahg. And I would imagine the same is true of Pip."

Lowrey looked at Pip, who nodded.

"Very well. I will pray to Cashi on the matter. It will be up to her what spells she gives me."

Location: Temple of Cashi, Londinium
Time: Mid-afternoon, 22 Cashi, 989AF

The spells Michael got were called *remember text* and they were new to him. They weren't all that powerful. They let the subject remember in detail a page of text that they had seen, in enough detail to copy it accurately.

This was going to take a while.

After reading the first few pages, the Temple of Cashi agreed to provide the spells in exchange for a copy of the pages that the subjects remembered.

It entailed Yahg or Betty having the spell cast on them then laboriously writing out the page. Both of them had other things to do so it was done when one of them was in town and not busy with something more urgent.

CHAPTER 9: WORD GETS OUT

Location: Temple of Noron, Magra, Nasine Empire
Time: Mid-afternoon, 23 Cashi, 989AF

Alfonzo Gabriel Panza, intercessor of Noron, was only a little bit bonkers. He occasionally had dreams in which the god spoke to him, and the knowledge those dreams had provided in the past had proven of great value to the temple and the empire. So, if he occasionally walked the halls of the temple or palace, speaking or even arguing with people who weren't actually there, it was accepted.

"I don't think it's important," he said to empty space. "Who cares what the god of merchants says? She has little more honor than the merchants who follow her."

Apparently, the air offered a reply because a moment later Alfonzo yielded the point. "I never said I wasn't going to report it. I just think it's silly."

A short silence, then, "Yes. I know if Noron thinks it's important, it's important. But you . . . Oh, never mind, we're here." He turned to the slightly overweight but otherwise fit woman who stood post outside the High Intercessor's door.

"I need to report to the High Intercessor."

"So I gathered," muttered the High Intercessor's secretary.

She knocked on the door and announced Alfonzo, who walked in without waiting for permission.

Along with the High Intercessor was his Imperial Majesty, Carlos of Nasine.

Carlos looked at High Intercessor Gonzales half in surprise, half in irritation at their discussions being interrupted. "Should I call my guards and have this buffoon taken to the dungeons under my castle?" he asked, not entirely in jest.

Maria Gonzales, High Intercessor of Noron, was a woman in her sixties, but still fit and active. She could still wield a sword, but only in the salle as a devotion to Noron these days.

"I wouldn't advise it, Majesty. I suspect Noron would be irritated if you were to lock up his Voice." She turned to Alfonzo. "What's so urgent?"

"I don't think it's urgent, but Noron told me and so I'm telling you."

Alfonzo went silent, and after a moment Maria asked, "Telling me what?"

"What?" He blinked. "Oh, yes. The god of contests says Cashi is getting aid from elsewhere and it could change the very nature of contests.

Which is just silly. Merchants know nothing of honor or the blade."

"There are other sorts of contests than blade against blade," Maria said. "What sort of aid and from where?"

"I don't know. Something about adding money and wealth to an economy. As for where, all Noron said was elsewhere."

Suddenly Emperor Carlos of Nasine wasn't looking bored or irritated. Emperors, as a class, are always interested in money. Even here in Nasine, where Noron was held as the most important of the gods, Cashi had a temple.

Carlos and Maria questioned Alfonzo, but didn't get much more. Apparently the information was going to the High Intercessor of Cashi at the temple in Londinium in the Kingdom Isles, and Cashi was excited about it.

Location: Tavern in Normanland, West Coast of Parise
Time: Mid-afternoon, 25 Cashi, 989AF

Captain Louis Gaston, the skipper of the freighter, passed the booklet across to the tavern keeper. It was twenty-five pages long and Louis had fifty of them in a box in the captain's cabin of his ship, *La Petite Rose*. The tract was on the process of making beer. It was the product of a tavern keeper named Glenda and a bard named Alvin. They'd combined their knowledge and written out a pamphlet on the techniques. It was supposed to produce a beer that didn't go sour nearly as fast. It was one of eleven such booklets on all sorts of useful things.

"I have ten more on other subjects if you're interested?" Louis knew that the tavern keeper would be interested. It was a nice tavern in the best part of the town of Normanland, which was the port and largest town in the county of Normanland in the nation of Parise.

Normanland and who owned it was the core of the ongoing war between the Kingdom Isles and Parise. The king of the Kingdom Isles insisted he'd inherited it from his mother. The king of Parise insisted that, no, it had gone to her younger brother. There were armies in the field not twenty miles from here, arguing the issue with sword and bow.

Louis didn't care one way or the other. He cared about selling these booklets to this tavern keeper, who had more books than a man of his means should have and was known to love the things almost as much as he loved gossip.

The tavern keeper looked at the booklet. Then he looked again. He took it over to a lamp and looked closer.

"Yes, Louis. I'll buy it and all the rest, but not unless you tell me honestly how this came to be. This isn't written. No hand on Earth could make every M the same, every Z identical to all the others."

Louis cursed under his breath. Then he sighed and explained about a day trip he'd made from Thash on the north coast of Scots to Callbridge and the strange things going on in that town.

The captain spent three days at the tavern as *La Petite Rose* was unloaded and he arranged for new cargo. Then he sailed away, completely unaware that the tavern keeper paid for his extensive book collection by being a spy for the king of Parise.

Three days later, the king of Parise knew about the business in Callbridge and the treasure trove of knowledge that was supposedly hidden in dwarven tunnels.

Location: Tavern in Therguria, North Coast of Doichry
Time: Mid-afternoon, 5 Dugon, 989AF

The wizards college in Therguria was one of the oldest in Centraium. In fact, it dated back to the time the Dwarven Empire had ruled Doichry. It had training for natural wizards and for amulet wizards, and in the last two hundred years had included the education of book wizards. The rumors out of the Kingdom Isles were disturbing, because if there were actually a cache of magic of that sort in the Kingdom, it really ought to be in their records. They had extensive records.

The chancellor of the College of Amulet Wizardry was going through those records using an amulet of past seeing. It let him see the pages as though they were new, not the better part of a thousand years old.

He wasn't finding much of anything.

The Dwarven clan who had owned that part of the Kingdom had been moderately successful miners and there had been a branch of the clan that made and sold magical items. Mostly for mining, but also for war, and even a few for farming, especially underground farming. But there was no great amulet maker.

There was a knock and the chancellor lost his concentration.

"Yes, what is it?"

"The expedition is ready to leave."

"Does Gunter think he's actually going to find anything by going there?"

The clerk shrugged his shoulders. "The pamphlets are coming from somewhere and the Royce lantern works, as does the air compressor and . . ."

The chancellor waved a hand in surrender. "True enough, but wherever they are coming from, it's not from the Gimli clan."

"So you think that it's some Kingdom Isles genius?"

"A Kingdomer? That makes even less sense." The chancellor snorted. "They're still wearing bones through their noses."

The clerk snorted a laugh, and they left the archives to see off Gunther and his companions, who would be taking ship to the Kingdom Isles to discover where the wonders were coming from.

Location: Royce Townhouse, Callbridge
Time: Mid-afternoon, 7 Dugon, 989AF

The doping that Fred Wilson, the alchemist came up with was producing electricity. It was selenium and some other chemicals that Alvin didn't have the names for. At least he didn't know what the names translated to in the periodic table that Tim Walters was familiar with. But the black silicate combined with selenium black amber and dragon's blood was producing current when exposed to light.

Fred was an amulet alchemist. He had no innate magical ability and he hadn't learned book alchemy. Instead he used enchanted beakers and other tools that had spells crafted into them to purify or mix chemicals. It made him much more effective than a 13th century alchemist from Earth would be, but it also limited him because the spells didn't require any understanding of why they worked. The spells were crafted into the containers that would then, with the right ingredients added, make potions of strength or floating or whatever. All he knew or had to know was how to craft a given spell into a given beaker. So he had not known what Alvin was after till they got the results.

Now, though, he had an idea. "What you want is a paint of shocking. That's really obscure."

"What's a paint of shocking?"

"It's an apprentice trick. It's not good for anything. You paint an object with it and leave it in the sun. Then when someone picks it up, they get a shock. Most apprentices know how to do it, but it's no good for anything."

"It is now. If we can structure the paint into the right pattern, we'll be able to get a lot of power from light. Enough to run the motors."

* * *

Later, talking with Freedric, they got to work on a spell that would paint the black silicate in a pattern and use microwires of gold, also painted onto the silicate, to connect the cells on the silicate panel so that they got a direct current to feed into the battery that would then power the airplane motor.

Location: Royce Townhouse, Callbridge
Time: Mid-afternoon, 3 Coganie, 989AF

It was actually a simple spell. It took a pattern painted on a large screen and duplicated it on a much smaller surface. Its effect was like photolithography, and now that Alvin and Fred had gotten the chemical mix right, Freedric had managed to work up the spell.

The glow lights that filled a room with bright sunlight were considerably brighter when they were surrounded by a globe two inches in diameter and the amount of juice that sort of light put out was a lot. Almost a kilowatt per globe.

It would charge the battery pack in about four hours, and the battery pack plus the four globes would power the engine for about fifteen minutes of flight.

It wasn't great, but it was good enough for a test of concept.

Location: College of Book Wizardry, Callbridge
Time: Mid-afternoon, 4 Coganie, 989AF

Professor of Magical Structures Daniel Alexander carefully tied off the part of the spell he was working on, then answered the knock. "What is it?"

"Sorry, Professor," Thomas McKendrick said, "but you asked to be informed. They have started installing the black bulbs in the air boat."

Air boat was Thomas McKendrick's term. Thomas was a contemporary of Freedric the Incompetent. They'd been in the same class at the college,

Thomas at the top, and Freedric near the bottom. They knew that Freedric called it an airplane, but Thomas had very little respect for Freedric, so he renamed the other wizard's works to what he felt was more appropriate. Frankly, and only in his own head, Daniel tended to agree with Thomas' assessment. Freedric was hardworking, but lacked Thomas' gifts. Or perhaps those gifts were in other places. If this gadget of his worked, it would be a real accomplishment.

Location: Mortemer's Tavern and Trinkets
Time: early-evening, 4 Coganie, 989AF

The thieves guild knew about the loading of globes of black into the airplane as soon as the college did. They had good reason to. Pip was a former member and so was Yahg. Alvin had been, if not a member, at least associated with the guild. But, much more important, there were at least three spies in town who were paying them for any and everything they could find out about what happened in the Royce townhouse and they were getting fairly complete reports from Yahg's younger brother, who was much smarter than Yahg.

Location: Glenda's Tavern
Time: early-evening, 4 Coganie, 989AF

The Doichry scholar sat at a table for the evening meal. "Any word from Alvin?"

"Not precisely," Glenda told him as she served up sausages and cabbage. "But there is a rumor that they are installing those photocells that he made."

"You know," Gunther said as he cut a sausage, "even if that plane never flies, the inventions in it are worth a fortune."

"So you've said," Glenda agreed. She'd never told the scholar about Alvin's new set of memories. It was a private matter. None of her business, and certainly none of this fellow's.

Location: Royce Townhouse, Callbridge
Time: Mid-afternoon, 8 Coganie, 989AF

Yahg, Pip, and Albert Royce arrived by carriage at Royce townhouse. Alvin had sent Yahg word as soon as they had the globes working.

"I still don't like the idea of Freedric in that thing on its first flight," Albert was saying. "We have soldiers for that. Risking Freedric—"

"Freedric is the only qualified pilot on this planet, Albert," Yahg said. "I was certainly never in a position to learn to fly." He was referring to John Kipler, though Yahg hadn't had any opportunity either.

CHAPTER 10: FIRST FLIGHT

Location: Field Next to the Call River, Outskirts of Callbridge
Time: Near Dawn, 9 Coganie, 989AF

The morning was crisp and cold, but there was no ice. Freedric checked the windsock. There was an intermittent breeze from the northeast, but no weather nearby.

Then he looked around. Word had gotten out. Half of Callgridge was out to see if Freedric the Incompetent was going to kill himself. The Skiff, as he had named the aircraft, was ready. It had a single main wing that was above the fuselage with one degree of dihedral in the wings. The dihedral effect of the high wing design added another effective five degrees of dihedral. The upper surface of the wing and tail were coated in the solar cells of the same type as the globes. They wouldn't add much juice, even on a sunny day like today, but every little bit helped.

He did his walk around. The plane had skids, not wheels. He didn't trust the field he'd be taking off from not to have gopher holes to eat one of his wheels. Besides, he knew a grease spell and he was going to cast it on the skids just before take off.

He didn't find any flaws. He didn't expect to. He'd checked it yesterday and the day before.

Then he climbed into the cockpit and turned on the systems. The batteries were fully charged and the stepper motors controlling the flaps, elevators, and rudder were all working fine. Alvin's—or Tim Walter's—knowledge of electronics had contributed a lot to the design, making the plane lighter and making it into a fly-by-wire airplane.

He climbed out and cast *grease* on each skid, then climbed back in and turned on the motor, pushing it up to fifty percent power and the plane skidded along the ground. He pointed it into the wind and watched the marker, feeling the wings bite and the skipping feeling of lift. He pulled back the stick and the tail flaps came up, pushing the tail down and he was flying. He straightened the stick and gained altitude at a slow upward glide.

At twenty feet H over G, he gave it another ten degrees up angle, then he was climbing at a good clip. He had to up the power to eighty percent to keep from stalling, but he was up and flying. At a thousand feet, he dropped the nose slowly, until he was barely gaining altitude, then banked into a slow left turn until he was slowly circling Callbridge.

He checked the battery. The Skiff was eating power. He was down twenty percent already. He really should bring it down before he let the batteries get too low, but he didn't. There was something beautiful about flying, especially this plane with the electric motor above and behind him. He could barely hear it at all. It was quiet and easy up here, almost like a glider, except he had power.

Hmm. He cut power back to fifty percent. He was starting to lose altitude, but at this angle of attack, he wasn't in any danger of a stall and he could go for a lot longer.

Gods, he loved flying.

* * *

Albert Royce watched the airplane slide across the field and lift into the air and in spite of everything, was shocked. He had thought he was ready for this. There were legends of magic carpets and pegasi that could take people through the skies and wizards who could fly on their own. He'd never actually seen one but they were supposed to exist. So, in theory, Freedric, with the extra memories of Jerry Garmon, should be able to do it.

In theory. Hypothetical.

Not.

Very much not!

In cold, hard reality!

Yet here it was. A man was flying in a device built by men and the man was a man he knew. He watched the device—oh, yes. Freedric called it the Skiff—lift its nose and start to go up faster. It seemed slow, but it was already little more than a dot in the sky.

Then he looked around at the crowd. If he was shocked knowing about Freedric's, Alvin's, Betty's, and Yahg's memories, the rest of the audience were worse. At first they just stared like he had, then they started arguing, insisting it was some sort of illusion.

A young man in the robes of a Callbridge scholar of the Magical Arts was insisting loudly to a professor that it must be an illusion of some sort.

The professor just stared at the dot in the sky, then ran over to the field and looked at the grass where the skids on the bottom of the airplane had crushed a path as the airplane slid across the field before taking off.

The young scholar followed him, still insisting it must be a fake.

"Shut up, Thomas!" the professor said. "Sorry lad, but do be quiet. I am trying to think. Look at the bent grass, Thomas. If it's an illusion, it's a very complete one."

Suddenly, a few feet to Albert's left, Yahg was laughing. It was a deep, roaring, almost angry laugh. And it went on as some of the onlookers turned their eyes from the dot in the sky to Yahg.

Yahg was looking at the scholars in the fancy wizards robes, then back at the airplane. It was turning now, circling Callbridge.

Great Gods! Albert thought. *It's halfway around Callbridge in only minutes.* Then, he remembered Freedric's predictions. "An airspeed between sixty and one hundred miles per hour." That prediction, which Albert had not believed, seemed quite accurate now. The Skiff was still making its slow loop around Callbridge and now it was heading back at them and it was getting lower too.

"Hey, you idiots!" Yahg roared at the now over a dozen people examining the bent grass in the field. "If you don't want Freedric's 'illusion' to land on your heads, you'd better get out of that field."

* * *

In the Skiff, Freedric was having a marvelous time, except that he was using up his battery way too quickly. Sighing, he circled back to land. They were going to have to improve the batteries or get more of the power globes. And he knew of no way. Freedric's musings on power output led to a new thought. *Of course, it isn't even a problem. Even a fairly basic jewel of light will give off light for several hours. Half a doz . . . What the hell are all those idiots doing in the landing field?*

He looked at his charge meter and realized he had enough juice for a couple more circles. "But if those gawkers don't get off the field I'm going to have a problem."

Jerry Garman was a qualified pilot. Not a test pilot, but he'd flown regularly for most of his life. He knew how planes operated, having designed, built, and flown several back on the Merge world. Freedric had all that memory knowledge and skill. He decided it was time to buzz the field. Fifteen feet H over G ought to be just about right.

He pushed the stick a little forward and added a bit of power to the motor.

* * *

People were looking at Yahg like a bear had spoken.

No one was moving out of the field. Albert looked back at the airplane. *Great gods!* It was coming right at them, and it was coming fast.

"Get out of the field, you idiots!" He added his voice to Yahg's. Betty and Alvin were also yelling now. A few of the people looked at them, then at the airplane, and started to move. But not all of them, not nearly enough of them.

The professor and the scholar were slow to react. They were still in the field as the airplane flew over them at a hight that appeared to be low enough to take off their heads.

* * *

Thomas McKendrick ignored the orc and the humans screaming about something. He was still trying to figure out how an illusion could bend grass stems.

Then Professor Alexander grabbed his robe and pointed. The illusion was coming back and it didn't look all that much like an illusion. It looked like some sort of winged javelin flying straight at him. While not actually an adventuring wizard, Thomas did have *fireball* and kept a copy of it prepared. In the moment, all he could think of was stopping that monster before it reached them.

If a fireball is crafted as a trap, it goes off where the crafter has set it to go off. If it's cast by a book wizard or from a rod of fireballs, it works a bit differently. A little seed of fire leaves the rod of fireballs or the wizard's finger, then proceeds along in a straight line until it encounters something solid or until it reaches the limit of its range. Then *boom*.

Even a dragon doesn't fly half as fast as the Skiff. Freedric wasn't traveling straight at the people on the field. He was buzzing the field. Pointing the plane so that it would fly above the field, not land on it.

To Thomas it looked like the plane was coming straight at him. He cast the spell using his pointing finger to guide the fireball.

He shot his fireball straight at it.

The seed of flame went under the Skiff, though it only missed by a couple of feet. It proceeded another ten meters at the speed of an arrow, then exploded behind the Skiff. It scared the heck out of Freedric, and a bunch of the onlookers.

In the meantime, the Skiff had overflown the field. An airplane goes up because it's pushing air down. The Skiff was just pulling up from a dive. A shallow dive, but a dive. It was traveling at upwards of a hundred and twenty miles per hour. The wind that slammed into the ground of the landing field and everyone standing in it wasn't quite gale force. Not quite.

It *was* strong enough to knock Professor Alexander, Thomas McKendrick, and several other people to the ground, and make the point that it was time to leave the field.

* * *

Yahg, seeing the fireball, charged, ax in one hand, and ran at the fallen wizards.

Professor Daniel Alexander heard the orc roar, looked up and saw the charge. In his youth, Daniel had been an adventuring wizard for a while. It was known to be a quick, if dangerous, way to gain skill and ability. Daniel wasn't given to panic. Nor was he slow witted. He was shouting. "We yield" at the top of his lungs before the orc was halfway to them. Which was a very good thing. Otherwise, someone would have died.

Which would have spoiled the day.

Using the dwarven-made magical ax, Yarg herded them off the field, cursing the idiocy of scholars all the way. Thomas McKendrick started to take umbrage several times and was silenced each and every time by the professor.

They got back to the edge of the field, where they were met by Albert Royce and two hastily gathered city guards, and taken into custody.

Next time around, Freedric landed with little incident. The grease spell on the runners had faded, so they provided more drag and a shorter landing distance than Freedric would have preferred, but he was belted in with chest straps and all he got was a slight bruise on each shoulder where the straps dug in.

He climbed out of the plane, and looked around to see that everyone was keeping their distance.

Then Yahg, Pip, and Alvin headed over, followed hesitantly by Fred Wilson, and Marcy Louise Caris.

"It flies quite well." He grinned at them. "What the hell happened with that fireball? You pissed at me, Pip?"

"If it had been me, you'd be toast. It was some scholars from the college of wizardry. Albert has them in custody."

"I guess we'd better go see."

"Not just yet," Alvin said. "Albert has things well in hand and there were a lot of people who were watching the flight. You need to talk to them."

"And say what?"

"One small step for a man, one giant leap for mankind," Alvin said. "Or something equally stirring. Look, Freedric, I didn't realize what this was going to mean and I should have. You're not some twentieth level wizard with a magic tower. You're a low to mid level wizard in a low magic world, and you just put Orville and Wilber's first flights to shame in front of a town full of witnesses."

Alvin was a bard, a singer, and a composer of ballads. He could do words and music and he'd been thinking about this, so they came up with some stirring, fairly meaningless phrases about the advances that were offered by the new technologies. Not just flight, but other sorts of transport, and even more uses.

Freedric spoke to the crowd, flubbing several lines, but the crowd seemed forgiving.

Then, with help from the crowd, they put the Skiff back in the warehouse and locked it up.

Location: Royce Townhouse, Callbridge
Time: Near Noon, 9 Coganie, 989AF

Albert took the mulled wine from the sim of his dead sister and cringed a bit. It still felt creepy. He took it anyway, sipped, and sighed. "I'm sorry, Freedric. I underestimated you. I believed you, and yet I didn't. It wasn't that I doubted you so much as it just all seemed so unreal that until I saw that thing in the air, I couldn't comprehend what it meant."

"Can you now?" Yahg asked. "On our world, it was just over half a century from the first airplane to the first man on the moon. Of course, this world has two moons, the Red and the Green, but the point is the same. Changes are coming and you can't possibly stop them, even if you killed the four of us and everyone who has worked on the airplane. That's more than twenty people, by the way."

Albert looked at the orc and grinned. "Settle down, Yahg. Not everyone thinks of their ax as a first answer to everything."

Yahg snorted in disbelief, but it was true. Albert would have been opposed to harming them, even if he'd thought it would work, and not just because he was increasingly fond of Betty Cartwright. Then suddenly he felt like he'd been gut punched. The airplane was proof. It was proof of Alvin's electronics, Yahg's maths, and general science. And most of all, of Betty's banking and accounting lore.

Albert wasn't a spy, but he was a successful man of affairs with a knighthood and lands in service to a king and noble lord. He recognized several of the people in the crowd today, not necessarily as individuals but by type. They were agents. Scholars, artists, diplomats, all those roles were taken up by the same sort of individual. The same guy who painted the duke's daughter's portrait also designed his fortifications, and often traveled to other courts to act as the king's representative in negotiations that might prevent, or start, a war.

Several of the folk who had watched that plane circle Callbridge had been just that sort of people. They were, at best, going to rush home to their respective kingdoms and report that the Kingdom Isles now had working aircraft that could carry people quite well. At worst, they were going to try to steal the airplane and kidnap Freedric, Alvin, Betty, and even Yahg.

Albert didn't have a warrant from the king to do much of anything. He couldn't order the lord mayor of Callbridge to do anything. It had been beyond his authority to have the two city guards take the fireball throwing moron into custody.

Ordering the lord mayor to put the warehouse and this townhouse under guard and protect Yahg with their lives was way beyond what he had the authority to do, but it was the minimum—the very minimum—that was needed.

He looked around the table. Freedric and Alvin were arguing weights and power outputs. Betty was listening, seeming to understand it all, and occasionally adding caveats about material costs, and the time and labor needed to craft a light spell.

Yahg was watching Albert, but apparently listening to the conversation because he asked, "What if you cast light on the inside of the photovoltaic globe?"

Which caused Freedric and Alvin to stop, look at each other, then start arguing again.

Yahg stood and gestured to Albert, and they went out of the dining hall into the front hall. "What's bothering you?"

"You four just became the most dangerous and valuable people in Centraium, not just the Kingdom Isles, *all* of Centraium. Maybe the whole world. The rest of the world doesn't know it yet, but it will. First in the Kingdom, then in Parise, then the Nasine Empire and the rest of Centraium. Assuming the Dragonlands and the Godlands, the Orclands and the Elflands are real, they will learn about it sooner or later.

"Do you realize we might be invaded just so that the king of Parise can get his hands on you four?"

Yahg looked at Albert, then slowly nodded. "Did anyone ever tell you, Albert, that you are a truly depressing person to talk to?"

Albert laughed. "The person who needs to know about this first and foremost is the king."

Yahg wasn't convinced. A person of his sort had little in common with the king of the Kingdom Isles. The general consensus was that King Arthur III was no King Arthur the Great, and as disillusioned with politics as John Kipler had been before the Merge, the sort of power that these feudal lords held over the common man was enough to turn the hard right Kipler in to an out and out commie. It wasn't even the power that bugged him most. It was the sense of entitlement, the notion that because of their birth, they deserved your loyalty and subservience.

"We've had this argument before, Albert. I don't owe you anything because you were born the son of a knight and I was born the son of a bone picker. Well, I don't owe your king anything either."

"I know." Albert grinned. "I'd say it was your wild orc blood, but I've gotten the same complaint from Betty, Freedric, and even Alvin. But you've never met King Arthur III. I have. Yes, he expects loyalty, but he gives it too. And he feels a strong sense of duty to the people of the Kingdom Isles. He is a good man, Yahg, as good as circumstances allow him to be."

Yahg wasn't convinced, Albert could tell, but after a pause, he asked, "What do you want to do?"

"I want to get in that airplane of Freedric's and fly to Londinium just as fast as it will take us. Then I want to sit down with Freedric and the king, and tell them what's going on."

"I thought you'd been giving them briefings on a regular basis."

"I have, but that's not the same as seeing that thing fly".

"No, I guess not," Yahg agreed. "At least not to you."

"And I haven't told them everything. I haven't told them about the extra set of memories that each of you carries. Now, I think we must. We need them to hear you and Betty, not a woman and a half orc."

They went back into the dining hall. Freedric and Alvin were still arguing about photovoltaic globes.

"Freedric, when will your plane be ready to fly again? How far can it go, and how fast can it get us to Londinium?"

"We don't know any landing spots between here and Londinium. If we were going as the crow flies and we didn't have to land, it would take about an hour, according to the best maps we have. It's eighty miles. Of course, those maps could be off by who knows how much. Also, there's a mountain range between us. It's not very high. I think the highest peak is no more than four thousand feet. The Skiff can fly over them, but climbing that high will use power and decrease the range. The Skiff's only good for about fifteen minutes of flight time, then we have to stop somewhere and let the batteries recharge."

"What about that recharge spell you have?" Albert asked.

Freedric grimaced. "It works, but crafting the spell takes over an hour, so we are still going to have to set down before I have the recharge spell crafted again. And trying to craft the thing while flying a plane? Forget it."

"So we'll have to find at least one open field, probably two, and possibly more."

"Sure. If we knew where to look," Freedric agreed. "But the right way to do it would be to map out the route, have the airfields ready, fly ten minutes, land, or perhaps cast *recharge* into the battery to add another fifteen minutes of flight time, then land at 25 minutes of flight time. If the meters were right, the Skiff has a cruising speed of about eighty-two mph so, we cover 35 miles per hop. At least three hops, and that assumes we can travel in something close to a straight line. So, an hour at each stop to craft recharge, so four hours to get to Londinium, if nothing goes wrong. Also, the Skiff isn't set up for instrument flying and we certainly don't want to be taking off or landing at night." He shook his head. "Give us a few weeks and we can probably be able to get you there in a couple of hours, but it's way too risky to try right now."

"It's a matter of relative risk, Freedric," Albert said. "What I realized when I saw that thing fly was that it changes everything. And the only way I can see to make that clear to His Majesty is to fly to Londinium and show him."

"Okay. But what makes it so bloody urgent?" Freedric asked.

"Right now, there is a wizard somewhere in Callbridge sending a magical message to his liege lord explaining that stealing that airplane of yours, and you with it, is worth starting a war.

"And I don't have the authority to guard it here."

It took more convincing, but Albert got his way. Then, while Freedric started crafting *recharge*, Albert went to see the Lord Mayor of Callbridge.

Location: Lord Mayor's Office, Callbridge
Time: Early Afternoon, 9 Coganie, 989AF

Sir David Munch, Lord Mayor of Callbridge, had spent the last hour putting out fires. Metaphorically speaking. He had two scholars from the College of Magical Studies in his cells after one of them had thrown a fireball at an eldritch device flown—that's right, flown—by another wizard. So the chancellor of the college was here to get his people out of the cells, and to lodge a complaint over their arrest. There was a delegation from Parise insisting that the eldritch device be impounded so that it might not be used against all the conventions of warfare.

"Sir David," his clerk said, "Sir Albert Royce is here to see you."

David grimaced. "Send him in."

The man walked in, "Sorry to disturb you, but I wanted to inform you of a few things."

"The time for that would have been before that device flew."

"Granted," Albert Royce said as David waved him to a chair. "The device is an airplane. The particular airplane is called the Skiff, because it's a relatively small airplane. And because that's what Freedric named it."

"That would be Freedric the Incompetent, who, according to graduate wizard Thomas McKendrick, must have stolen it, because no one of his limited abilities could possibly make it."

"That's the fellow," Albert agreed. "Though Thomas McKendrick's assessment is even worse than his aim. I am assuming that Thomas McKendrick is the idiot who, after wandering onto the airfield, threw a fireball at the airplane and thankfully missed."

"Yes. It was self defense. So he and the chancellor of the College of Wizardry insist. Now, why didn't you inform me?"

"Because I drastically underestimated what the airplane flying would mean. It was just Freedric's project, one of several projects that have been in process in the last months."

"Yes I know about the projects coming out of Royce house: the drum printers, the Royce lamps, the steam pumps for draining mines, and more everyday." Sir David Munch, gave Sir Albert Royce a glare. In terms of title, they were of equal rank. On the other hand, David was a lord mayor and Albert was a confidant of the king, or at least a confidant of one of the king's confidants. "What do you want of me, Sir Albert?"

"I have no authority to order you to do anything, Sir David. I know that."

Sir David held up a hand. "I asked what you wanted of me, Sir Albert. I'll decide what I can and will do."

"Good enough. I want Royce house guarded. I want to make sure that Yahg, Betty Cartwright, and Alvin the bard are safe and not harassed."

"And your brother and sister?"

"Them too, but that is a personal matter. Yahg, Betty, and Alvin, well, if the king had seen what I saw this morning, he would be ordering what I am asking."

"What about Freedric the Incompetent? He's the one who supposedly built the airship. At least, that's what is being claimed."

"That nickname is a bit outdated. Ask the workmen at the shop where it was made. Freedric is the designer. But you won't need to guard him, for within the hour Freedric and I will be in the Skiff and gone. Where we are going is to go no farther than this room until we get there! Is that agreed?"

"Yes, if you insist."

"We're going to Londinium just as fast as the Skiff can get us there. The king needs to see the airplane flying over Gwiniver Castle."

"You are going to get in that thing while Freedric the Incompetent flies it . . . tries to fly it to Londinium?"

"Freedric assures me that it's quite safe," Albert said with a grin.

"Let none doubt your courage, Sir Albert," Sir David said. "Or your gullibility."

Sir Albert laughed and they separated on good terms, each to his own duty.

Location: Field Next to the Call River, Outskirts of Callbridge
Time: Two Hours From Sunset, 9 Coganie, 989AF

Everything had taken longer than desired, so they were only going to be able to do one flight before the sun went down. Fortunately, they were going to be traveling east southeast so the sun would be behind them, not in their eyes.

They got to the field and Betty had put blankets and a basket of cold chicken in the back seat of the plane. They pulled the plane out and oriented it, then Freedric cast grease on the skids again, and they took off.

"It's a little sluggish with the extra weight," Freedric muttered as they took to the air.

It didn't feel sluggish to Albert. Once they were up, they turned southeast and found themselves flying over forests and hamlets, pastures and fields of wheat and rye. Small fields and small pastures.

Fourteen minutes into the flight with the battery level reading low, Freedric feathered the engine and let the plane glide. Then he unhooked two connections and cast *recharge* on the battery. The spell was instantaneous, returning the battery to a fully charged state. He reconnected it to the electrical system of the airplane and brought the engine up to 80 percent power.

"Between that and the power globes, we should have another fifteen minutes, but I'm starting to look for a place to land now. I want to be down and safe before the sun sets. I'm going to want to put out wards."

Albert agreed.

Twelve minutes later, they passed beyond a chunk of forest to a wide plain that was apparently mostly pasturage for sheep.

Freedric circled it twice, then landed. The landing, Albert discovered, was rather more exciting than the take off.

Albert set out the blankets and their dinner, while Freedric used his magic to place wards around the plane. Animals would avoid the wards, and even people would be uncomfortable approaching them, but it wouldn't take much of an act of will to force your way past them. They were more a warning than an actual wall.

Location: Mortemer's Tavern and Trinkets
Time: One Hour From Sunset, 9 Coganie, 989AF

Paul knocked on the door and gave the password. He knew that his older brother had the memories of that other person. In spite of that, Yahg was still Yahg. Yahg had been the family's protector almost as long as Paul could remember. He'd always been Paul and Elizabeth's protector. What was strange was having him as Paul's advisor as well.

The door opened and Paul went to the table where the thieves' council were sitting. There was a fifth member of the council again, another thief, Jimmy the Hand.

"I told you it would fly," Paul said.

"You did," Mags agreed. "But you didn't tell us it was going to fly off."

"That's because Albert Royce got a hair up his bum. He's afraid that someone's going to start a war to get the Skiff."

"That's crazy," Mack the Cudgel said.

"No, Mack, it's not," Pete the Cat said with a grin. "I should have thought of that. Royce is a clever one, he is." Then he looked at Paul. "Freedric's gone, but Alvin is still here."

"Freedric's the one who matters." Mags said. "Pip and Alvin just aren't that smart, whatever the workers in that airplane shop of Freedric's say."

No one even mentioned Yahg, which was just the way Yahg wanted it. Paul was caught between being pleased and resentful, that in spite of the evidence to the contrary, the thieves guild still thought Yahg was dumb as a stump.

"Where did they fly off to?" Mags asked.

"Londinium."

"You said it didn't have the range to go all the way to Londinium." Mack said, looking like he was going to come after Paul for lying to them.

Paul was scared and resented being scared. "It doesn't. They are going to do it in three, maybe four, hops about thirty or forty miles each."

"So three or four days?" Mags asked.

Paul shook his head. "Freedric has a recharge spell. I told you that. It will take him an hour to craft it after they land, then they will be able to take off again. But they won't be flying at night, so they'll probably reach Londinium some time tomorrow. Pip put a picnic basket in the plane. I think she's gone soft over Albert Royce."

Tommy the Black growled. He really did hate Pip.

"So that thing is going to be in Londinium tomorrow," Pete said. "If we're going to act then we need to do it now."

"I told you Alvin and Pip don't matter."

"We can still sell them to the spies and wizards," Tommy said. "After seeing that thing fly, they'll pay good silver for them." He was grinning.

Paul shook his head. This was what he was *really* here to tell the thieves guild. "The mayor has put guards on Royce house. No one goes in who doesn't belong there. They questioned me when I left. Albert had a talk with the mayor."

"Damn!" Tommy said. "I'm starting to hate that bastard."

"Forget it, Tommy," Pete said. "You go after Albert Royce, you'll find yourself trussed up like a chicken and dropped on the mayor's front stoop."

"Forget all of it," Mags said. "Alvin was right. They are all off limits. And, Tommy, that includes Pip." She gave Tommy the Black the sort of look that would give Paul nightmares if it was directed at him. Mags liked poisons, the sort that killed you slow.

* * *

Paul left the guild with five coppers for his trouble and headed back to the townhouse to tell his big brother what the guild of thieves had decided.

CHAPTER 11: ROYAL RESPONSE

Location: Field in Northern Wiles
Time: Near Dawn, 10 Coganie, 989AF

It had been a quiet night and at dawn Freedric was at his books, crafting *recharge* and two copies of *grease*, which left him little room for other spells. Then they climbed aboard and were off again. By now they were into the foothills of the Spine mountain range. Freedric decided to get some altitude so that he would be able to look for a flat place to put the plane down. He wanted to get as close to the spine as he could, so that going over the mountains wouldn't be too much of a strain. They only went about twenty miles to find a place that was near what looked like a pass between the mountains.

Albert wasn't sure, but he thought that it was Donnybrook Pass and the landing place, which was near a small town that was where Count Donnybrook made his place. It was also where he collected the tolls on those using his pass.

They landed and five minutes later were surrounded by a troop of cavalry. Very nervous cavalry.

Albert waved to them, and said, "I need to have a few words with the count. In the meantime, please don't disturb the wizard. He gets irritated if you bother him."

Given that they'd arrived in a flying machine, that was enough to ensure that Freedric wasn't bothered while he was crafting his spell.

* * *

A few minutes later, Albert was climbing down from the borrowed horse. Then he heard Victor Allen Donnybrook ask, "What are you up to, Albert? This had better be the king's business or you're going to owe me your house in Londinium as passage fees."

"I will happily pay whatever fees His Majesty decides I owe you, Victor, but it's just me, a fairly irritable wizard, and our means of conveyance. That hardly seems worth my Londinium house."

It took a bit of talking, but he left Victor Allen with a nominal fee and a promise that future flights wouldn't bypass his customs station, as long as the fees were reasonable. They had a breakfast of sausages, eggs, and bread, then took off again.

They headed southeast and when Freedric cast *recharge* on the battery, Londinium was in sight, less than ten miles away.

They circled the city, then landed on Covent Green, just three streets from Gwiniver Castle.

Just minutes after they landed, they were surrounded by a troop of the King's Own. A fairly irritated troop, which was a good thing, because after flying over a city with a population between eighty and a hundred thousand people there was a crowd around the King's Own that were surrounding the airplane and its occupants.

Location: Gwiniver Castle, Londinium
Time: Late Morning, 10 Coganie, 989AF

King Arthur III was sixty-seven years old and looked it. His hair was snow white and thinning, and his beard was just as white, if thicker. On the other hand, he was well dressed and moved with a spry grace. He was also apparently irritated.

"This was the only way you could think of to let me know that your friend's device worked?" He glared at Albert, then shot a glance at Freedric. "Congratulations, Wizard. It seems the tales of your incompetence were somewhat overstated."

Freedric noted a twinkle in the king's eye that made him think the king wasn't quite as upset as he seemed. "I was a slow starter, Your Majesty."

"Made up for it now, right enough. And I don't blame you for the grandiose pageant that Albert here, put on. He was managing me. Or trying to," he added ominously at Albert. "I've sent for Lord Tenhoks, who is going to have a few choice words for you as well. But in the meantime, you two come with me to my private study. We need to talk about this."

* * *

By the time Lord Tenhoks, Duke of the South March, arrived ten minutes later, His Majesty had a clear idea of the capabilities and limitations of the aircraft, and how those limitations might be adjusted in the future. He was a bright man, well studied, and willing to listen. He didn't understand aerodynamics after ten minutes with Freedric, but he did understand that Freedric understood aerodynamics. And not from reading some dwarven tome.

"How do you know this?" The king held up a hand as Lord Tenhoks came in. He waved him to a chair, then continued to Freedric. "This isn't something you figured out on your own over a weekend of thought. Your knowledge, your terms and knowledge of them . . . No, this is something that you have studied for years. So where did you learn it and how?"

Freedric looked at Albert, who shrugged agreement.

"Don't look at him. I'm the king, not him. Now answer my question."

Freedric did. But he couldn't resist adding that Jerry Garman was from a nation without any sort of nobility, and even in the countries that had kings, the kings reigned, but didn't rule directly.

That led to a discussion of the right of blood inheritance and whether it was as much an illusion in this world as it was in Jerry's.

"The king is the land, Freedric. I've felt it a bit all my life, but more since Excalibur was placed in my hand."

Freedric didn't know. It might, in a world where magic worked, be real. Or it might be an honest belief reinforced by the placebo effect. There was no way for him to know.

They went back to airplanes and the other inventions, and Betty and Yahg's concern about the effects of introducing new products without introducing enough money to balance it.

"Yes," Lord Tenhoks said. "Albert, here, has been harping on that for some time now."

"And if the airplane is real, we must assume the rest is real as well," King Arthur said. "That was the point of this stunt of yours, wasn't it?"

Albert shrugged. "It's true that discussion is a lot easier to ignore than an actual airplane flying over Londinium, Your Majesty, but that wasn't the only reason. Two days ago it was all concentrated in Callbridge. A wizard out of Parise or the Nasine Empire, even Dorchry, could end the whole thing. But today, such an attack would have to reach Callbridge and Londinium. It would be too great a risk and much less certain of outcome."

"But who would know?" His Grace, the Duke of the South March demanded.

"Everyone, Lord Tenhoks," Albert said. "There were representatives from all over in the field outside Callbridge where the first flight was made. By now the Emperor of Nasine knows. So does King Louie of Parise, and the Baron's Council of Dorchry. Heck, by now I expect the dwarves know about it."

"Leave off, Peter," King Arthur said. "Right or wrong, Albert thought it was what he had to do. And I'm not convinced he was wrong. I saw that airplane flying over from the balcony of the royal apartments. It was startling. You were taking a chance, Albert. I had to talk two of my wizards out of trying to take it out with a lightning bolt."

"That was what convinced me that Albert was right, Your Majesty," Freedric said. "A wizard from the college at Callbridge shot a fireball at me as I was trying to land on the maiden flight. I wasn't sure how long it would be before someone with better aim tried it."

"Well enough then. What's done is done. We will now discuss what is to be done about it."

And they did for the next several hours. The two wizards with the lightning bolts were brought in and Freedric got to describe how the airplane worked. How batteries worked and electric motors worked. And how Alvin the Bard knew much more of their workings than he did. Then for the next three days Freedric briefed the Royal Society of Magic on the workings of aerodynamics and electronics.

He was inducted into the Royal Society, something only the Royal Society could do, not even the king.

Then, after a short stop at Sowford University, where again he got to explain aerodynamics and electronics, they flew back to Callbridge with royal warrants.

On the trip back, Freedric started teaching Albert Royce to fly.

Location: Townhouse of Duke Dandridge, Londinium
Time: Late Morning, 10 Coganie, 989AF

There was a meeting in Gwiniver Palace and Duke Ronald Alen Dandridge wasn't invited. It was hardly a new thing. The old fool who held Excalibur didn't trust Ronald and never had. Arthur's mother, the former queen, hadn't trusted Ronald's father either, even though he was her younger brother. Or perhaps it was *because* he was her younger brother. He should have been the king, not Boudicca the queen. And Ronald should be king, not Arthur. He would be if the Kingdom Isles worked the way the Pariseians worked.

In the months since Albert Royce had come into the king's favor, dozens of new devices had come out of Callbridge. Useful devices usually, but disturbing devices. Devices that were upsetting to the social order. And Arthur, who was more of an old woman than his mother had been, had done nothing to suppress them or even to make sure they stayed in the hands of the nobility, where they belonged.

From his balcony he could see the aircraft surrounded by the king's own. Everyone in Londinium had seen that thing fly over and Albert Royce climb out of it.

Such a device shouldn't exist and if it had to exist it should belong to the right sort of people. Royce was barely a knight.

He turned around and went back inside. Something would have to be done.

Location: Field Next to the Call River, Outskirts of Callbridge
Time: Near Noon, 19 Coganie, 989AF

Someone at the Royal Society, it turned out, did indeed know *shrink item*. Further, it turned out that a shrunk lead acid battery works just fine in its shrunken form. They had made four more batteries while at Sowford and shrunk them all, giving the Skiff a flight time of two hours. Plenty to go from Londinium to Callbridge in a single flight and give Albert stick time as well.

The landing field was clear with city guards to keep everyone off and Alvin and Pip were there to greet them. So were Thomas McKendrick and Daniel Alexander. Alvin was watching them both. So were the city guards.

Albert climbed out of the Skiff first and stretched. Flying as a pilot was an interesting combination of boredom and terror that had a tendency to leave Albert with stiff shoulder muscles.

Then as Freedric climbed out, followed by Magister of Magic, Eric Simonson, who'd been sitting in the back seat watching them both like a hungry hawk eying a fat mouse. Something that hadn't helped with Albert's muscle strain.

Albert went over to Betty while "Call me Eric," a squat, jovial, balding fellow continued to follow Freedric as Freedric made his post flight inspection.

* * *

Albert reached Betty and took her hands then lifted them and kissed the back of them. While in Londinium, he'd had time to see his daughter and was informed that she missed Betty and he should marry her before she got away. A sentiment that Albert found himself in complete agreement with. Assuming he could convince Betty Cartwright, for whom he had letters of ennoblement, to do such a daft thing.

"Hello, Betty," he said. "The king wants you in Londinium to run the Kingdom Isles bank."

Betty blinked in surprise.

Albert kept talking. "Emily misses you."

That brought a smile.

"She says I should marry you before you get away. I agree, except I can't think why you'd agree to such a thing, since the king has made you a countess with a county on the southern coast." He started to babble something even sillier, but Betty interrupted by kissing him, and he couldn't say anything for a while.

She took a breath and said, "I think Emily is smarter than either of us."

"Me too!"

"I assume this is the newly made Countess of the Isle of Green," said Eric Simonson with a twinkle in his eye. "Wise of you, Albert, to secure your position before all those wolves in Londinium find out that she's to head the Kingdom Isles National Bank, which will have authority from the crown to make loans and mint and print currency."

"What?" Betty squeaked.

"Albert was right about the effect of the airplane in providing our bonafides," Freedric added. "His Majesty proved quite decisive."

"What about Parliament?"

"The king will make it a royal bank, if you can't get Parliament to go along," Albert explained. "But he wants you to see if you can convince the commons to endorse the plan. The levies and taxes needed to pursue the war with Parise have left the House of Commons a bit restive."

"Perhaps this isn't the best place to discuss all this," said Sir David Munch, the Lord Mayor of Callbridge.

"An excellent point," Eric said, looking around.

The Skiff was being pulled into the warehouse where it was built. There were now four wizards just on the edge of earshot and at least two dozen people were here, having seen the Skiff circle the town as it came in for a landing.

"Why don't Albert, Countess Green Isle. and the Lord Mayor here, go to Royce house and talk politics," Eric continued. "Meanwhile, Freedric and I will discuss what is and isn't magic with those fellows over there." He pointed at the wizards. "But I'm going to want to see your airplane shop later, and you know that the king wants more airplanes just as soon as you can make them." Then he looked around like he'd lost something. "And where is this Alvin the Bard who understands electrics? Him, I really want to talk to."

Everyone went off to talk and they spent the rest of the day discussing their part.

The workmen at the airplane shop were all quite pleased to learn that their temporary jobs had become both permanent and prestigious. Eric wanted to see everything and expressed his enthusiasm for the skill and craftsmanship of the carpenters and tailors who had made the wings and body of the Skiff.

Daniel Alexander followed along, leading the scholars from the Callbridge College of Magical Arts, and fielding questions from Eric about what he understood of what kept the airplane in the air, how it turned and banked, what dihedral was and how the dihedral effect was changed by the positioning of the wings. All while Magister of Magic, Eric Simonson, demonstrated to everyone present that Freedric and Alvin understood what was happening and why, that the craftsmen in the shop understood some, and that the scholars of magic understood almost none.

Daniel found it humbling and a bit irritating. Thomas McKendrick found it humiliating and the other scholars of the Callbridge found it illuminating. There were ways of doing magic that didn't involve what they had learned of magic. Ways that Freedric knew. At this point, not even McKendrick was willing to call him "the Incompetent."

Location: Royce Townhouse
Time: Noon, 19 Coganie, 989AF

The sims and magical servants served a lunch of smoked ham and spiced apple preserves. By now Albert could almost ignore the images of his younger brother and sister who brought them the food.

They discussed the bank and the House of Commons.

House of Commons. Called by the king in each location, was called to select one or two members of the gentry to send to the commons. That included belted knights like Albert and the Lord Mayor or sometimes prominent property owners who lacked any title, even knighthood. They met together a few weeks out of the year most years. How they were selected was up to the location that sent them. Sometimes they were elected, sometimes selected. But most subjects of the kingdom weren't in Parliament and hadn't voted for anyone who was. They were called the Commons because they were not of the upper nobility, which started with barons. Betty Cartwright, aka Pip the thief was by His Majesty's hand, made Countess of Green Isle, which put her in the House of Lords. They were still discussing the factions in the House of Commons when the others arrived late that afternoon.

* * *

Magister of Magic Eric Simonson came in speaking with Alvin and Daniel Alexander about the uses of electricity. Albert quickly ordered the two sims to their recharge chambers. The fact of his siblings demise was not something that he had shared with his liege lord or the king, much less these people. Albert found the whole situation a shame to the family. At the same time, he couldn't bring himself to destroy the sims who were all that was left of his brother and sister.

Betty, and by now she mostly thought of herself as Betty, watched Albert. He was a stiff and proper man, that much was certain. But changing that wasn't something that she was going to accomplish in one go. So she went and joined in the discussion in the front room, while the sims retreated to the coffin-like structures that were used to recharge them.

"How long will the next airplane take?" she asked, fairly confident of the answer.

"Less time than it will take for Freedric to teach a pilot," Eric Simonson said. "Fred Wilson already had battery packs built for two more airplanes. It was simply an issue of weights that was preventing their use. And the craftsmen at Freedric's shop have many of the struts and supports already made."

"Piloting is the issue," Daniel Alexander insisted. "It should be limited to wizards and wizards able to craft *recharge* and for that matter *shrink item*. Unless you want the batteries to return to full size in the middle of nowhere. We have no idea yet what effect the charging and discharging of a battery will have on the durations of the *shrink item* spell."

"That won't be possible," Albert said, joining them in the front room. "His Majesty asked Freedric to teach me to fly, and I am going to be spending a lot of time flying back and forth between Londinium and here. Also, he wants there to be one plane in Londinium at all times as soon as possible."

"Well, His Majesty was poorly advised," Daniel Alexander said. "Nothing against you, Sir Albert, but you simply lack the knowledge—"

"You don't need to know how to repair a plane to know how to fly one, Master Alexander," Freedric said. "At the moment, Albert has more hours of stick time than anyone but me."

Daniel subsided, but not happily. And the crowd adjourned to the dining room, where magical servants, not including the sims, served dinner. And the discussions of airplanes and electronics continued.

Location: Glenda's Tavern
Time: Evening, 19 Coganie, 989AF

Gunther had spent over ten gold pieces in the last week. He begged, bribed, and bought everything he could find on airplanes and electronics. He had bits and pieces, as well as drawings and descriptions. He ate his sausages and beets with care so as not to spill on the papers. He would be leaving tomorrow to go to the coast and hence back to Doichry. He was fairly confident that given what he knew, he could build an airplane and one that would fly. The electric motor would be an issue, but he thought he could get around that with a pull spell of some sort that would pull the plane through the air. There were similar spells that pulled barges up and downriver. Not that it would be safe. How Freedric had learned to fly without killing himself was something that Gunther had been unable to learn. He examined the notes on the electric motor and the batteries. Used in the airplane he was planning or not, they would be useful.

He was tempted to stay and learn more, but he had strict instructions from the Lord Chancellor of the university in Therguria, so home he was going.

* * *

Glenda watched the man. He'd been an open-handed guest, and she rather liked the man in spite of his accent and obvious knowledge. He wasn't particularly arrogant and was friendly in his way. But the truth was she'd miss the extra income more than the man.

And she knew from her fellow tavern keepers that there were other curious travelers brought by the airplane.

Location: College of Magic, Callbridge
Time: Evening, 19 Coganie, 989AF

Thomas McKendrick had an excellent memory and high intelligence. He also came from a privileged background. He was the younger brother of a landed knight and his early interest in matters intellectual had been indulged by the family. He'd had tutors from an early age and worked with them to expand his knowledge and understanding of magic and the way it worked. He'd entered the College of Magical studies at 14 and been at the top of his class from the moment he'd arrived.

Freedric the Incompetent was just the opposite. He wasn't stupid and his family wasn't poor, or he'd never have been admitted. But he wasn't brilliant the way Thomas and his friends were and he hadn't had the special tutors that many of Thomas' friends had. Freedric was easily distractible and his mind wandered, which was downright dangerous when crafting or casting spells.

All through school, Thomas had felt contempt with only the least hint of sympathy for his less adept classmate. If Freedric had stayed the less competent wizard Thomas knew in his undergraduate days, Thomas would probably have been willing to help him out. Perhaps even recommend him for a job if it didn't require a *real* wizard.

But Freedric had not remained incompetent as he was supposed to. Instead, he and a bard had introduced two new fields of magic and Freedric had been admitted to the Royal Society of Magic, which had left Thomas a lap and a half behind.

Today had been humiliating, but educational. He knew what an airfoil was now and how it worked. He knew what streamlining was and much more about how wings worked. The moment he got back to the college he'd gone directly to the spell books. There was a spell, Adreana's Gossamer Wings. It produced a set of bird wings that grew out of the caster's back. It was a difficult spell, but Thomas was quite a good wizard.

With his new understanding of magic, he realized how the spell could be used without the flapping part. Modifying a spell like this was no simple task, but Thomas was a skilled wizard and quite motivated.

Location: Normanland, Camp of Prince Edward
Time: Evening, 19 Coganie, 989AF

Prince Edward of the Kingdom Isles was a tall, blond man in his early forties. He led an army of knights and yeomen in an attempt to retake the Normanland from the Crown of Parise. They had made some initial progress, but then the Dauphin of Parise, the heir to the throne of Parise, had been taken ill and a canny old soldier from Lorraine had taken control of the Parise forces, who had then refused battle on the open field.

And now this. He looked at the letter from his father again.

"Stay where you are. Help will be coming in a few weeks. Don't risk your army or yourself until you hear from me.

Arthur III, King of the Kingdom Isles."

He crumpled the note in his fist and was immediately tempted to take his army and ride out in search of the Dauphin and attack. Edward was the second of his father's sons. The eldest, Richard, had died of the bloody flux when Edward was just a lad. So he'd spent his life in competition with a ghost who, as Arthur remembered him, was all that was good and right in a prince.

This war had been Edward's chance to display his valor and skill at war. And he had, until the idiot Dauphin got sick.

He sighed and went back into his tent, cursing the muddy ground and the Dauphin, the Marquise of Lorraine, and his father.

Location: Normanland, Camp of the Dauphin, 9 Miles Northeast
Time: Evening, 19 Coganie, 989AF

Jules wasn't any more pleased with the letter he got from Louis of Parise than Edward was with the letter from King Arthur III.

He was in a good position, on a hill with stone formations, making attacks on his position difficult, and saw no reason to move from his comfortable position.

"Jules,

You must end this, and quickly. The Kingdomers have a new magical device. Several new magical devices, that will change the balance of power in their favor. One of them is a flying carriage that will let them observe your forces from the sky and drop wizard bolts, fireballs, lightning bolts, and something called bombs on your forces from above. You have to end this and push the Kingdomers off Centraium before they can bring their new magic into play.

Louis, King of Parise

It was insane, but it was also the king's orders. Cursing, Jules set about getting the army of Parise ready to move.

Location: Field Next to the Call River, Outskirts of Callbridge
Time: Midmorning, 20 Coganie, 989AF

"No, that's all right, Albert. I've never flown an airplane. I'll be perfectly happy in the back seat," Betty said. Then she climbed into the small plane. It was designed to be a four seat aircraft with a small luggage compartment behind the cabin. Once she was in and settled with some toys for Emily in the other rear seat, Albert got into the left seat in front. The Skiff had two sets of controls. The left hand side set could be turned off by the right, so Freedric could take over if needed. Freedric got in and taxied the Skiff into position, then said to Albert, "Okay. You're going to take us off. First, you'll want to up the power to 80 percent, then you watch our airspeed. When it reaches 60 mph, you pull the stick back, but just a little. You want about five degrees up angle until we get a bit of altitude, because this is a tricycle design, not a taildragger. You don't want the tail touching the ground." He continued to discuss what was going to happen in what order, then told Albert to start.

Albert followed instructions, not without a bobble or two, but well enough, and in a couple of minutes they were in the air and rising at a slow pace.

"My plane," Freedric said and flipped a switch that shifted control to his controls. Then he pulled back on the stick, and they were climbing. He pushed the power to 95 percent and the Skiff climbed faster. Five minutes later they were at five thousand feet, almost a mile up. Freedric put them in level flight and turned the controls back over to Albert, then talked him through turns and banks and even had him stall the aircraft twice so he would know how to react. That was the reason that they were so high up, so there would be time for Albert to recover from mistakes or, failing that, for Freedric to take back control of the aircraft and save them if Albert really screwed up.

Even as Freedric taught Albert the basics of flying, they were traveling roughly southeast toward the mountains, and Freedric showed Albert and Betty how the landmarks appeared different at different altitudes. An hour later, they were flying over the mountains known as the Spine, and a few minutes later Freedric, not Albert, brought them into a landing.

The landing field was just outside the walls of Londinium, and right where the king had said he was going to place it. The skids gave them the standard short, sharp landing and there was a carriage waiting.

There was also a fussy little man named Colin Farington.

"Oh, crap," muttered Albert. "Already?"

"What?" Freedric asked, concerned.

"Sir Colin Farington is the chief clerk of the king's purse." Albert looked over his shoulder at Betty. "I was hoping we would have a little time before your new duties descended. But . . ." He hooked a thumb over his shoulder at the approaching gentleman. ". . . there they come."

Freedric laughed and opened the door. He stepped out of the plane onto the cold, wet ground of the landing strip. The ground had frozen the night before, but the weather, a balmy forty or so degrees, had melted the ice before they landed.

He didn't quite slip and fall.

Albert got out, pulled the seat back forward, then helped Betty climb out of the back seat, steadying her on the slippery grass.

Betty reached up a hand and got a grip on a wing strut, then turned to face the little man who was carefully mincing his way forward with an arm full of ledgers.

"If you expect me to examine those here," Betty said, pointing with her free hand, "you're sorely mistaken. I will examine them in an office where neither they nor I are in danger of falling into the mud."

Sir Colin Farington stopped dead in his tracks, then almost fell. "Oh, yes!" he said. "Of course, so sorry, Countess Green Isle. But His Majesty insisted that you be made familiar with the privy purse as quickly as possible."

Betty, with the experience of twenty years of dealing with often irate banking customers, smiled a warm and friendly smile and said. "Quite right, but as soon as possible is as soon as the books and I are in a place where both are safe from mishap."

* * *

Three hours later, Albert was at Royce house, Freedric was getting ready to fly back to Callbridge with a Captain Nigel Fairbanks as his passenger and flight student.

And Betty, for her sins, was locked away in a room in Gwiniver Palace, going over the king's books. They were, to put it bluntly, a mess. The king's purse was the accounts of the whole of the Kingdom Isles. That wasn't unique. It was just how it was done in the here and now. There were records and accounts for everything from the army in Parise to the last royal dinner. There were records of taxes owed and fees received.

And there wasn't a computer—or, for that matter—an adding machine anywhere she knew of.

"How in the hell did we manage to build an airplane before we built an adding machine?" Betty muttered, then made a note. She went back to the books. There was a knock on the door.

"His Majesty wants to see you," Sir Colin Farington said.

Sir Colin's attitude seemed to be changing. At first, he'd been resentful that she should be placed in such a position. Resentful, but still intent on carrying out the king's wishes. But as he'd watched her going over the books and checking and double checking, he'd come to sort of accept her as someone who at least understood the value of getting it right.

"And I have no experience dealing with kings," Betty admitted, adding to herself, *not in either life.*

* * *

His Majesty introduced the Chancellor of the Exchequer, Lord John Gray. He was not a fussy little man. He was a scholar, educated at Sowford, but he was a member of the upper nobility and had been his entire life. He was a tall man, broad shouldered, with dark eyes, and graying hair. Once the door was closed, he asked, "So how will you spin straw into gold for us?"

"Rumplestilskin, Rumplestilskin, Rumplestilskin," Betty replied promptly. The story was a fairytale in both worlds and Rumplestilskin was the name of the dwarf who made the girl the offer.

Lord John laughed, stood and bowed. "So tell us about a national bank?"

Betty told them, wishing Yahg was here. Her knowledge of banking was better, but his knowledge of the federal reserve system was better than hers. She talked and insisted that the absolute first thing that must be seen is that the king trusted the bank with the crown's purse.

"All of it?" King Arthur asked.

"That would be best. Most of it, certainly. It was good that I got a look at your books, Your Majesty. We can separate out day to day expenses and have at least part of the money to pay them stay here. The most important thing is to make it clear that the king be seen to trust the bank."

"So first we give you all the king's money, then you will make us all rich," Lord John said with a bit of a bite in his voice.

"Oh no. In fact, you're never going to give me so much as a copper piece. The treasury will be held wherever the exchequer determines under the care of guards he and the king trust. I'm never going to touch a coin."

"But you said—" Lord John started.

The king held up a hand. "What are you going to do, Betty?"

"I am going to create paper money and issue debt."

The discussions went on and it was very late by the time she got to Royce house.

CHAPTER 12: THE BATTLE OF HOGAN'S HEAD

Location: Normanland, Camp of Prince Edward
Time: Midmorning, 28 Coganie, 989AF

"They're coming," the prince's aide said.

It wasn't a surprise. Both sides had scouts. They'd known when the army had started to move and one of Edward's bards was magical and had a spell of *invaded dreams.* He'd informed a counterpart in Londinium and gotten back word that help was coming.

"Form the men. We will follow the king's orders." *For the first charge anyway,* Edward added to himself.

* * *

Duke Jules was an uncle of the dauphin and wasn't a fan of this war, the present king, or the dauphin. He was, however, loyal to his older brother and unwilling to start a civil war while there were Kingdom troops on Parise soil. But he didn't like the battle plan that the king's orders had forced upon him.

One attack he would make, then he would fall back and try to draw Edward into a pursuit.

* * *

Sixty-one miles away, Freedric and Yahg climbed into the Skiff. The back seat had been removed and replaced with a rack of ten twenty-pound gunpowder bombs. Word had just arrived from a network of magic users.

"I hate this," Freedric said. Freedric had been an adventuring wizard for at least a little while. He at least knew how dangerous combat could be. Jerry Garman had been an engineer his whole life. He'd never seen a shot fired in anger.

Yahg grinned. "It's the cost of doing business. The king is giving us his support and we are expected to earn it. Come on. It's not like these babies are Fat Man or Little Boy, and this is hardly the Enola Gay. Heck, we may actually decrease the casualties if we break the Parisesens quickly enough."

Having checked the rack, Yahg climbed in and turned to Freedric. "Let's go, Oppenheimer. We're the good guys."

Freedric took the fairly heavily loaded Skiff off and pointed it east to Hogan's Head, not quite the closest place on Centraium to the Kingdom Isles.

* * *

An hour later, they saw the armies.

"Be careful, Oppenheimer," Yahg said. "We don't want to drop our bombs on the wrong army.

"Stop calling me that," Freedric muttered.

"Then stop beating your chest and tearing your shirt," Yahg said. "I have a lot less reason to be loyal to the Kingdom Isles than you do, and I'm not bitching. This is a war. We didn't start it, but we are both in the service of the Kingdom Isles. If the world we are trying to build is going to get built, it's going to have to be built in the Kingdom Isles, and it can't do that if Parise wins this war."

They knew the range of fireballs and lightning bolts and neither was much good at a thousand feet. Neither, for that matter, were bows and arrows.

Timing had turned out well. The Parise army was starting its advance. They had an excellent view as the army moved forward. The command group was near the rear, so that it could see the battle and exercise command and control.

The bad news was they had very little practice. The bombs were black powder with caps that were magiced to make a spark when the bomb hit the ground or anything else hard.

As the Parise army moved forward. They flew in from the north coast of the peninsula and Freedric slowed the Skiff to just above a stall about forty-five miles per hour indicated air speed. Yahg leaned out the side window, looked through a sight that had been clamped onto the door for this, and dropped the first bomb. It hit long, a good thirty feet past the command group.

The bomb plowed into the ground, then exploded, shooting a blast up at the unprotected bodies of the horses. Horses screamed and died, bucking in their death throes and the Pariese knights looked over, then up at the bird of death flying over. It turned and started to come back.

* * *

On the ground Duke Jules stood his ground and shouted at his captains to stand fast. The army was at risk. If they saw their commanders run, the planned retreat would become a rout.

The death bird came back and bows and arrows shot into the sky in a cloud. The cloud never came near the death bird, but rained back into the army that had fired it, killing more Parisean troops than the first bomb had.

This time Yahg had four bombs, two in each hand as he leaned out the window. The first he dropped early, the second half a second later, then the third and the fourth.

They bracketed the command group and it scattered, leaving Duke Jules on a wounded horse, trying to control his army.

* * *

Prince Edward wasn't happy. He didn't like the help he was getting. It seemed dishonorable. At the same time, he was a pragmatic man and he knew that his father wouldn't be happy if he failed to use any advantage. He started giving orders.

* * *

The Skiff dropped all twenty of its bombs, then turned back to the Kingdom Isles. By that time, the Parisean army was a mob and Edward and his archers were in range. The flower of Parisean heraldry died at the Battle of Hogan's Head, just as they had died at Agincourt in that other world.

But much of the credit went not to Prince Edward, but to the airplane and its crew. That didn't please the prince. But the fact that a week later, the Kingdom owned most of the Normanland peninsula and had a clear road to Ifle did, and it pleased his father more.

By then Freedric and Yahg had landed the Skiff among the Kingdom forces and spent days scouting and disrupting any Parisean formations.

Location: Normanland, Camp of Prince Edward
Time: Midmorning, 2 Timu's Time, 989AF

Prince Edward climbed into the right hand seat of the Skiff, and Freedric into the left hand seat. Yahg was in the back seat with a pad and paper, for this was a scouting mission, not a bombing run.

The plane took off. Prince Edward wasn't afraid of heights. He could stand on a battlement and look down without any more than caution. Somehow, flying in a plane was different. That difference was apparent from the moment they left the ground. But Edward was a brave man. He held until they were over a thousand feet up before he lost it altogether. Then he grabbed the right hand controls, which were deactivated. When that didn't work, he tried to grab Freedric.

That would have worked at least to kill them all, but Yahg reached around from the back seat and grabbed the prince and held him. And for the next twenty minutes, while Freedric flew the airplane, Yahg held the Prince of the Kingdom Isles tight and talked to him. He didn't speak gently, for Yahg wasn't a gentle man and neither, whatever the law held, was Prince Edward. Instead Yahg spoke of reputation and power. Of this one flight being the only one that the Prince would ever need to make, but that he did need to make it and to be seen to climb out of the Skiff after they landed. "Not be dragged out because you panicked and I had to knock you senseless."

Eventually, after a small eternity, the plane landed and Yahg released the prince. He turned like a cat with his dagger out, and Yahg just looked at him. Then the two very hard men stared at each other. Edward knew that Freedric was in the other seat. He even knew that the book wizard probably had a spell that could kill him. But this wasn't about Freedric. He was just a wizard. This was about Yahg. An orc who had had the gall to lay hands on the heir to the throne, and who had been right to do so, for even through his rage, Edward knew that Yahg's actions had saved his life. And, which was more important to Edward, his reputation.

Slowly, Edward's anger cooled. These two men held his reputation in their hands. "What do you want?"

Yahg didn't pretend to fail to understand. He grinned a hard, cold grin and said, "A knighthood."

Edward looked at him, and started to laugh. Then, still laughing, he turned to Freedric. "And you, wizard?"

Freedric honestly didn't understand for a moment, and when he did, he was tempted to say "nothing." But he knew that Edward wouldn't accept that. He was also tempted to say "a knighthood," even though wizards had their own system of ranks. So finally, he said, "Spellbooks."

"Done," Edward said to Freedric, then to Yahg "And done for you too, orc. It's not even hard, given what the two of you have done to the Pariseans. Now, I will never set foot in one of these vile contraptions again and how shall we arrange that?"

"Best to stick to the truth as close as we can," Freedric said.

"You prefer a horse to carriages or airplanes," Yahg added. "Not everyone likes to fly."

Three days later, just before they flew back to the Isle of Wiles, Edward knighted Yahg for his service to the crown, making him the first orc or half orc to be knighted in the Kingdom Isles.

Location: Field Next to the Call River, Outskirts of Callbridge
Time: Midmorning, 3 Justain, 990AF

The four days of Timu's Time had passed in celebration in Londinium, and Betty was still there, working up the design of the plates to print the money, while negotiating with the House of Lords and the House of Commons how the Kingdom Bank would be organized and who it would report to.

But Freedric and Albert were flying into Callbridge for an extensive period of flight training, after which the Skiff would be making the trip from Callbridge to Londinium every day, while the new airplane would be flown by Sir Yahg, and would work with Prince Edward's army.

Yahg's family was in shock and very worried. Also, it was a life knighthood, so it wouldn't go to his children if he ever had any, or his little brother if he didn't.

Still, it was freaking them out. Even if it went away later, it had pushed them from bone picker, at the bottom rung of Callbridge society, to just outside its top rung. There were perhaps two dozen landed knights who made their home in Callbridge and none of them would be inviting Yahg's family to dinner. But there were over a hundred propertied persons who were not knights, but yeomen, and as the father, mother, brother, and sister of a belted knight, Yahg's family actually outranked them now.

Most of those people weren't going to invite Yahg's family over, either, but some of them knew that Yahg's father Forton was now employed at the aircraft factory, and his brother and sister worked in the Royce Townhouse.

The plane landed and Paul, Yahg's younger brother, came out of the factory to help move the plane inside. "Is it true?" he demanded as soon as Yahg climbed out of the plane.

"It's true," Yahg confirmed. Most of his green fur was hidden by his new clothing, acquired in Londinium at great expense, but necessary given his new status.

"Yes," Albert said. "It's true. His Majesty wasn't expecting Edward to do that, but since he did it so publicly, he was unwilling to gainsay it." Albert was quite conservative in his views, and whatever his personal feelings about Yahg, he wasn't at all sure how he felt about the precedent. On the other hand, he knew exactly how Betty felt about it, so he was keeping his mouth diplomatically shut.

Paul, in short pants and no shirt, even on this cold day, attached a rope to one of the struts, then with the help of three other workmen they started pulling the Skiff into the building, Paul's green fur almost glowing in the morning sun.

Justain was the coldest month of the year and most of the workmen were bundled up against the chill, but not Paul.

The half orc girl who came out as the Skiff was being towed in wasn't displaying any green fur, just green hair and green eyebrows over a square face. She smiled at the group. "Master Freedric, there are books from the College of Wizardry. Cases of them." Elizabeth, Yahg's sister, was showing a great interest in book wizardry. She'd had little opportunity for education until quite recently, but she was trying to make up for lost time.

Freedric smiled at Elizabeth. He thought she had the mind for wizardry; it took more than an interest in books and reading. In spite of his desire, it didn't come naturally to Freedric. He'd had to work very hard to acquire the habits of thought that were necessary to craft spells. Elizabeth was working just as hard as he had, but had a great deal more natural talent for book magic than Freedric had had before the Merge. The Merge and Jerry Garman's memories had helped, both because Jerry's mind was naturally more focused than Freedric's and because of the insights that Jerry's knowledge of physics and engineering provided. The horrible truth was Thomas McKendrick was probably right in his expectations of Freedric's potential if the Merge hadn't happened.

Which didn't make Thomas any less of an arse for his attitude.

"Those will be the books Prince Edward was arranging."

Location: Royce Townhouse, Callbridge
Time: Noon, 3 Justain, 990AF

Yahg settled down to lunch with his mother, father, and younger brother. His sister Elizabeth was upstairs with Freedric, examining the books.

"We should send for Elizabeth," Yahg's father Forton said irritably. Pop was a lot more concerned about Beth than he was about the boys. And that concern didn't always please Elizabeth. For the most part, Yahg agreed with Pop on the matter. But not in this case. He knew Freedric and he'd known Jerry Garman. Neither man was the sort to take advantage of Beth. If there was any seducing going on, it would be going the other way. And Freedric would end up asking Pops for Beth's hand if it got that far.

If it were to get that far it would take time. It was way too early in their relationship for a romance to develop. Freedric was teaching her magic, and that was enough for now. It wasn't like they'd be taking her to the Callbridge College of Wizardry any time soon. Knighthood or not.

"Leave them be, Pop."

"I know you're a knight now, Yahg," Pop said. "But I'm still her father."

Yahg laughed. "It's not that, Pop. But I know Freedric. He's not going to take advantage."

"Maybe not," Paul said. "But I'm not at all sure that Beth isn't up there taking advantage of him."

"You mind your mouth, boy," Pops told Paul, but he looked worried. So did Mom, but only a little. Mom had been the one who'd chosen an orc over family and society. And she'd done it with her eyes wide open. She figured that Beth would make her own choices. That was how she'd raised all her kids.

"You say you know this Freedric?" Mom said. "Tell us about him."

Yahg did, including about Jerry. Hiding his new intelligence from his family had never been an option. They knew the old Yahg too well. That was part of the reason that he wanted them in the house, and away from the kids they'd run with before the Merge. There was a small orcish community in Callbridge, made up of the orcs and a few of the very poorest humans. It was the children of those that his brother and sister had played and worked with. The truth was that the only reason Beth hadn't been raped by now was because it was well known that Yahg would kill the rapist. She was an attractive and bright girl, and if she set her hat for Freedric, she'd probably get him. "He's a cautious man, more hard working than talented. Jerry, now, is a different story. Jerry's been an engineer for decades. He's not good at people, not suave or dashing, but he can build things."

"That's for sure," Paul said. Paul was deeply impressed by Freedric's airplane and wanted to be a pilot. He was going to be, too, assuming once he got up in the air, he didn't get airsick or anything.

Yahg, with John Kipler's memories of Earth, was much more familiar with flight controls, so he'd picked up flying pretty quick.

"Quiet, Paul," Pop said. "Let your brother talk."

Paul rolled his eyes, but kept his mouth shut while Yahg told stories about Freedric and Jerry Garman. Then he said, "I'm going to want to take Paul with me when I go back to the front."

That changed the subject quite adequately. They were concerned about Beth, but taking a fifteen year old boy, especially a half orc, to a warzone was crazy. And they had a point, but Paul would have things in his favor. One, he would be going as a mechanic for the Skiff and a pilot trainee. Still, it took a lot of convincing to get his parents' permission.

* * *

Upstairs, Elizabeth was examining the books which were ostensibly a gift from the Society of Magic in Londinium. A gift that had been encouraged by His Highness, Prince Edward.

"I need to do something nice for the Society," Freedric muttered as he examined the books.

There were spells that produced wings and spells that called an ethereal steed that could fly. Most of them were above his ability, but some were spells that he could learn and some were spells that he could use to improve the airplane's function in take off and landing.

That wasn't the only magic. He was reading about a spell of lifting plate that allowed a plate or shield to float above the ground and move at the direction of the caster. The plate or shield could support a weight of up to a hundred pounds for a wizard with who could craft it, and up to three hundred pounds for a really skilled wizard. Freedrec translated the instructions in a game of WarSpell, a fifth level wizard could lift a hundred pounds and another ten pounds for each level over fifth the wizard had. Even a 25th level wizard couldn't use it to lift an airplane, but if he built it into an airplane and allowed it to age adequately, he might be able to use it for landing gear.

"Hey, it's a battery spell," Elizabeth said.

Freedric looked up.

"Well, a battery charging spell. At least, I think that's how it makes the metal band heat up."

Freedric went over and looked at the spell over her shoulder. He thought she was right. As he put a hand on her right shoulder while his head was to the left side of her head, and he read the notes on the procedures and, yes, what the spell did was produce a current possibly alternating, possibly direct, through a piece of metal and it was the current that heated the metal. "You're right," he said, nodding. "It's a third level spell, too, and it can be put in an item."

He squeezed her shoulder. "Very good catch, Elizabeth." Then he stood back up and went back to the book he'd been working on.

Beth still felt his hand on her arm. And she realized that he wasn't hitting on her. He'd been treating her as a colleague. It made her feel good, and at the same time, a little disappointed that he wasn't hitting on her. It was that disappointment that made Beth realize that she might actually be interested in the man as something other than someone to teach her magic.

Location: Palace, Ifle, Parise
Time: Noon, 8 Justain, 990AF

Louis IV was shocked that Edward had made an orc a knight, life title or not. He focused on that outrage because of what he was having great difficulty facing. His army was shattered. The Kingdomers had a firm foothold in the Normanlands, and an open path to Ifle.

Something had to be done to stop them, but Louis didn't have a clue what. In spite of its coastline, aside from fishing boats, Parise was a country of the land, not the seas. Its gods were the gods of the harvest, of wine, and food, Barra being first among them. Among the nobility, Noron held great sway, but the official gods of the kingdom of Parise were Barra, Grapo, and Lussi. Flying was not really in their line. Nor was the winning of wars.

"An orc?" he demanded of the air. "Has Edward lost all sense of propriety?? Of station and class?"

Location: Palace, Magra, Nasine Empire
Time: Morning, 15 Justain, 990AF

Emperor Henry III listened as his seneschal read the report. He was far sighted and the words on a sheet of paper tended to blur. Having a clerk read it to him was easier and let him concentrate on the message, not on deciphering it. His wife, Queen Margarita of Cascoia was shaking her head as the reports from their agents in Parise made it clear that the airplanes of the Kingdom Isles could do more than scout from the sky.

"We should attack Parise!" Margarita said. "We have many a cause bellum and with the Kingdomers taking Normanland from him, Louis IV must be pulling all his forces north."

That was Margarita, always ready for another fight. Henry was less enamored of land conquests and more interested in expanding the empire through trade and shipping. "And what if our attack causes our royal cousin Louis to make common cause with the Kingdomers, or almost as bad, what if Parise collapses as a nation then is conquered entirely by the Kingdom Isles and we find their ships off our coasts and their armies on our northern borders?"

"What do you want to do, husband? Wait for one side or the other to win, then fall on us?"

"No. I intend to send embassies to both Louis and Arthur. And I intend to have airplanes of our own before we step into a war we can't win. Airplanes and the bombs they dropped." He looked over at the seneschal "That was what they were called, the amulets of fireball that the airplane dropped? Bombs?"

A quick look at the report, and the seneschal nodded. "Yes, Majesty. Bombs. But apparently it's not just bombs. We have reports from Londinium that the alchemical powder that fills the bombs can be used to make something they are calling cannon."

"Canon like a temple edict?"

"They add an N to the spelling. C A N N O N, but yes, it borders on sacrilegious."

"And what do these cannon do?"

"No one is certain, but it's said they will work like a ballista or a catapult and throw rocks against a castle wall to bring it down."

"What is the point? We already have ballista and catapults?"

"It's said they will be more powerful," the seneschal said. He knew better than to be meek before his queen. Margarita didn't respect weakness.

The discussion continued and by evening Henry and Margarita had come to a compromise. They would send an embassy to the Kingdomers and the Parisens offering to broker a peace. But they would also move their forces to the northern border in a position to move to the support of Louis, move against Louis in support of Edward, or take whatever other action seemed good, depending on how the embassies did. They would also send more spies to Callbridge to discover how airplanes worked and, if possible, to hire away some of the workers in the airplane factory.

CHAPTER 13: REVOLUTION, INDUSTRIAL

Location: Royce Townhouse, Londinium
Time: Noon, 13 Banth, 990AF

Betty Cartwright came into the house still talking to her assistant. Sir Robert Forsith was a member of the House of Commons, a burgher of Londinium, and the person that the House of Commons had chosen as their watcher in the Kingdom Bank.

"The money is now being printed and I think that we can be confident that it will be a while before the forgers catch up with our printing techniques," Betty was saying. "Hi, Emily. I'll be with you in a moment. So what I want to do is start getting the bank notes out to the public."

"Yes, but how? No one is going to take them."

"They will if the House of Commons insists that all taxes are paid with them."

Sir Robert Forsith tripped. Betty, with Pip's reflexes, reached out and kept the man from falling, but it was a near thing.

"His Majesty will never agree."

"His Majesty has agreed," Betty told him. "Go have a talk with the banking committee in the House of Lords. They have agreed too."

"Yes, Countess Green Isle," Robert Forsith agreed. Then he left and Betty squatted down to see what Emily was up to.

Emily was up to a small business. With the cooperation of the cooks, she and some of her friends were setting up a cookie and tea shop on Baker Street. Eight years old was more than a little young for that, but Emily's nanny was also involved, as were the nannies of the other girls on the block.

For the next hour, Betty went over the cookie and tea shop plans with Emily and got her assurance that she would accept royal bank notes.

* * *

There was a knock at the door and a maid went to open it. Alvin the Bard entered, followed by Albert Royce. There were now three airplanes. One was in Parise, being flown by Yahg. One was based in Londinium at the disposal of His Majesty, who liked flying and used the plane on a regular basis to travel around the Kingdom Isles, visiting Scutes and Eirie and impressing the heck out of his nobles. The third made the trip from Callbridge to Londinium on Monday from Londinium to Callbridge on Tuesday, and repeated, taking only Sunday off. Albert was the pilot of that plane and insisted that the system worked.

He spent a day in Callbridge working on the businesses there, because it turned out that neither Freedric nor Alvin were particularly talented at matters of business. Then he spent a day in Londinium, setting up copies of the Callbridge businesses in Londinium. Between the tools that Freedric and Alvin had introduced and the king's favor, both sets of businesses were flourishing, and the productivity of both cities were increased. Londinium, by perhaps five percent. It was a much larger town and many of the crafters were reluctant to adopt the new ways. In Callbridge it was up almost twenty-five percent. And both towns were seeing prices drop as production outpaced the money supply.

"Hi, Daddy," Emily said. "Betty has banknotes ready."

"Really?" Albert lifted an eyebrow. "The Commons?"

"I just sent Bob Forsith off to put a bee in their bonnet."

"Well, the shops in Callbridge will take it. At least, ours will, and that should get the ball rolling. Of course, people can't spend it unless they have it, and I have no notion of how to get them to accept it."

"I want you to discount silver, and gold coins against it. You can take copper at face value, but I want you to insist that a silver coin is only worth nine coppers because of testing costs, but paper notes are worth face value."

"People aren't going to like that."

"I thought about adding a copper to the value of a silver note, but it would be expensive and His Majesty wouldn't agree. Neither would the Lords. I think I've actually convinced His Majesty that the paper notes will have real value as long as we treat them like they do."

"What about the Lords?" Alvin asked.

"About a third of them," Betty said. "Fewer in the Commons, but His Majesty has agreed that he will accept taxes paid in paper money. In fact, he's gone one better. He's going to insist that taxes only be paid in bank notes. So to pay your taxes, you will have to take your coins to the bank, where they will be assayed to ensure that they haven't been clipped and that they are pure enough to be accepted without discount, then pay a fee for that service and collect your banknotes, which you can then use to pay your taxes."

"That's not going to make my fellow knights happy," Albert said.

The discussion continued as they all adjourned to the dining room, then Emily told her father about the business that the little girls on the street were starting and informed him that they would be insisting on bank notes.

Location: Royal Society of Magic, Londinium
Time: Mid Morning, 13 Banth, 990AF

"It's not proper magic," Sir Reginald said. "And I don't just mean the airplanes, though they are bad enough." He looked around the alcove just off the main lecture hall of the Royal Society.

"I don't think Freedric ever said it was," said Carl Vincent Abernof.

"That's not the point, Carl."

"Then what *is* the point?"

"The loss of art. Worse, the displacement of art by Freedric's mass production. Who needs a *rock to mud* spell when you can use his black powder to blow a hole in the side of a mountain? Who needs a chill spell when you can buy a refrigerator? And you *will* be able to buy a refrigerator. John has confirmed that compressing a gas increases the temperature. Releasing the pressure cools the gas. With the electricity that that bard is touting, you will be able to power the pumps to compress the gas and remove the heat. The art and craftsmanship of magic is threatened by Freedric's engineering."

The bell rang and they entered the main chamber where Lord Albert Commings was about to give a talk on sulfuric acid and lead to make lead acid batteries, and using magic to shape the lead and charge the batteries.

As he listened to the lecture, Carl Vincent Abernof realized the problem with Sir Reginald's argument. Magic and science simply mixed too well. Every new innovation that Freedric or Alvin introduced also introduced the possibility of new spells that could be developed and crafted.

And yet there was truth in the complaint as well. Yes magic could make and charge a battery, but you didn't need magic to do either of those things. Machines and tools could do them just as well and often more easily.

It was then that Carl realized the real core of Reggy's complaint. It was that engineering competed with magic. That it threatened the status of wizards. Carl was honest enough to admit, at least to himself, that that prospect bothered him as much as it did Reggy.

Location: Glenda's Tavern, Tanners Street, Callbridge
Time: Near Noon, 25 Banth, 990AF

Glenda wouldn't have taken the paper, but Boots wasn't someone you argued with.

He was a mugger and he scared her. So she poured the drinks and served the food and took the pieces of paper.

* * *

It was hours later when she looked up as Alvin the Bard knocked on the bar. She knew of his change of circumstances and he'd been by a few times, but never to play. Now he had with him a satchel.

"What can I do for you, Alvin?" Glenda asked.

Alvin pulled more of the bills out of the satchel.

"Not you too! Boots was here earlier insisting that I take that paper as though it was silver."

"Boots?" Alvin demanded. "Where would he get paper money?"

"Where Boots gets anything is something better not to ask about."

"True enough." Alvin smiled a friendly smile as he put the bills back in the satchel. "But if you already have bills, what you need to do is take them to the bank and open an account."

Glenda felt her mouth fall open. "You've lost your bloody wits, Alvin, if you think the likes of me can deal with that bank of Pips."

Pip, who was now known as Betty Cartwright, was a bleeding noble. Not even a knight. An actual noble. A countess.

"If you have bank notes, you can open an account. You can pay your taxes in bank notes."

"I don't pay taxes. I pay rent," Glenda said. The only people who paid taxes were people who owned property.

"Your landlord pays taxes and you pay the town fees. And all of that can be paid with the paper money."

He opened the satchel up again and pulled out a sheet of pressed paper, something he called cardboard. It was printed on one side with bank notes. A copper piece, a silver piece, an electrum piece, and a gold piece. Each note was square and had a picture of King Arthur on its face, and the denomination printed, plus several words and a complex design in three colors. "This is the paper money that's real. Is this what Boots gave you?"

Glenda pulled the bills from the waste basket where she'd put them. She compared them to the cardboard pictures. There were two silvers and a half a dozen coppers.

"Is that real?" If that sign was accurate, the paper money she'd had forced on her by Boots was worth five, maybe ten, times the price of his food and drink and he'd eaten a lot and drunk more than usual."

"Yes. It's going to prove as good as gold, and better than gold coins."

Glenda looked at him, then moved down the bar until her face was close to his. She whispered, "Is this from those other memories?"

Alvin nodded. "In that other world, almost no one used gold or silver as money. It was all paper and it worked as well as coins ever have."

It took some more persuasion, but Glenda agreed to get herself a bank account at the Kingdom Bank, Callbridge branch.

While they were talking, there was a *boom*.

Location: Steam Press, Tanners Street, Callbridge
Time: Noon, 15 Banth, 990AF

The press used steam to lift a weight and drop the weight on leather to cut and shape it in one stamp. The owner of the shop wasn't the company owned by Albert Royce and the wizard. The owner was Francis Alan Hodges, a member of the landed gentry, an esquire, not a knight, but also a man of business.

He'd hired away a worker at the stamp press factory down the way and was using the same technique the stamp press factory used to shape and cut steel, to shape and cut thick leather into things like boots and heavy leather armor.

Francis paid them no royalties and got no help from them. He was quite proud of that. He watched the stamp come down and the very hot steam being squirted into the gap to keep the leather from burning while it was shaped, then decided. He told the smith that he'd hired away from the stamp press factory to increase the steam pressure.

"I don't know, boss. They have—"

"I don't care what they have, we need to lift the arm faster."

Sighing, the man added more heat to the steam tank. It was a pot boiler because tube boilers would have taken too long. They were working on it, but for now everyone in Callbridge was using pot boilers.

As metal heats up, it becomes more malleable and welds become weaker. The heat in the firebox was nowhere near enough to melt steel or iron. It was just hot enough to make the weld between the top of the pot boiler and the rest of the pot a little bit weaker. It also made the steam hotter and that increased the pressure that would have been easy to see if they'd had a pressure gauge or if they'd had a steam release valve. They had neither. The first indication of a problem was when the weld failed and the top of the steam kettle blew through the ceiling and then through the second floor and the roof, and continued up two hundred feet more.

Then the steam flashed out and killed everyone in the building by replacing all the air with superheated steam. The collapse of the building was nothing more than an afterthought.

* * *

Alvin was running toward the building. He shouted for Glenda to gather up anyone she could find to help. The steam explosion had put out the fire in the fire box, but it would take time for them to learn that. For the first minutes and hours, there was just work and fear as they pulled lumber away and found bodies. There were six of them. They found Francis Alan Hodges, his brother George and his wife, as well as three employees. They also found the steam press and a dozen other devices that had been copied from those developed by Royce Enterprises.

Francis' cousin, the heir to the family property since Francis had no son, sued Royce Enterprises. The suit was thrown out once Albert showed the magistrate that Francis had not had permission to use any of the devices.

But the explosion was one more case that a conservative faction in the House of Commons was using to try to outlaw the innovations that Albert, Freedric, and Alvin were introducing.

It wasn't just the wizards who were nervous about the new magicless magic. It was knights and property owners, burghers and more than a few intercessors.

Cashi, they had on their side. And Prima was giving those of her intercessors who got spells a new spell that helped identify illnesses so that they might be more readily treated.

Location: Glenda's Tavern, Tanners Street, Callbridge
Time: Early Evening, 5 Barra, 990AF

There had been changes in the last five months since Glenda had started accepting paper money. The ice box held chilled meats. It also held ice from the ice house that had an electric refrigeration system to make tons of ice each day. That ice was then carried to ice boxes in homes and businesses, so there was cold pasteurized milk and cold vegetables, cheeses. And cold beer. All of which had improved the quality of Glenda's food and drink. It was still on Tanners Street, but the tables were new and Glenda had a full house most nights.

Meanwhile, the conversations were changing. As Glenda passed out fried chicken, a new recipe that she'd gotten from Alvin, she heard factory workers arguing about the House of Commons and the new bill to outlaw steam engines on the basis of how dangerous steam explosions were.

"Oh, I'd be fine with them if everyone was using the tube boilers that Royce came up with, but they aren't. There was a steam explosion in Bristol last month. We should stick to electric and use wizards to charge the batteries like they do here." The speaker was a large, brown skinned, red haired man. His name was Tom O'Rork and he was from Eirie. He was making decent wages, but the news from Eirie was sobering. The property owners, who were mostly from Wiles, were setting up factories with little regard to safety and even less to patents.

"Sir Albert has loosed the dragon and there's no putting it back in its hole," said Diego Harrak from southern Centraium. "Even if your House of Commons institutes such a law, it will have no sway in Moorland. The Nasine emperor cares less for the Moorish slaves than your Wiles nobles care for Eirie peasants. All such a law would do is give the advantage to the Nasines."

"What do we care about the gods cursed Nasines?" O'Rork insisted belligerently.

"You'll care enough when Carlos sends his steam powered ships to land his armies on Wiles," Diego insisted right back.

Glenda stepped over to the table and put her hand on O'Rork's shoulder. "I'll ask you to keep it calm or take it outside, Tom."

Tom O'Rork turned, then his face calmed. "Aye, Glenda. If this refugee from Moorland won't see reason, he won't."

"He might have a point, though. Last we heard, the king of Parise has made a treaty of mutual defense with Nasine."

Glenda couldn't read, but she did get the *Callbridge News* and had it read to her by Elizabeth Fortonson, the sister of Yahg, the knighted orc and pilot. Glenda hadn't been friendly to the orcs before what Alvin called the Merge, but since then, knowing that Elizabeth was studying book magic with Freedric, Glenda had made friends with the family. They were still trying to find their way into their new status, and so was Glenda.

She had connections. Alvin and Yahg's family, but the world was changing so fast. As she went back to the table, she wondered how Yahg and his little brother Paul were doing in the war zone, and how Pip was doing on the Isle of Green.

CHAPTER 14: THE ISLE OF GREEN

Location: Isle of Green, Kingdom Isles
Time: Mid Morning, 6 Barra, 990AF

Betty Cartwright climbed out of the airplane and looked at her estate. The Isle of Green was a small island just off the southeast coast of the Isle of Wiles. It was one of a series of islands that formed a sort of blockage that limited the waves in the Great Bay. Until Betty got it in fief from the king, it had been a royal preserve that held a fishing village and rather more goats than people.

There was a strong wind blowing from the southwest and it was warm. The pilot got out, looked around and said, "What a dump."

"My, aren't we getting fancy," Betty said to Paul, Yahg's little brother.

Paul was a sixteen year old half-orc who looked rather less orcish than his famous older brother, in spite of the fact that he had a lush coat of green fur. From their memories of the game, Betty and Yahg had a good knowledge of orcs' semi-plant fur and the effect it had on orcish health. They had shared that knowledge with their relatives and Paul slept under a magical plant light when he could. That had improved his health as well as that of the other orcs and half orcs in the family.

So not only did he have a lush, if short, coat of green fur, he was also full of energy in a way only a healthy teenager can be. He made Betty feel tired just looking at him.

He set about tying down the airplane. The Isle of Green was a windy place, having lots of grass, but not much in the way of trees. He and Betty could see that there were people coming toward them.

* * *

Mayor Michael Jones was not looking forward to this. He knew about it, of course. They got a boat from the mainland most weeks. And after butchering they got an actual ship to take the wool and meat to the mainland for sale. So he knew about the grant of the isle to this Countess Betty Cartwright, who had no family anyone knew of, but was in charge of the new bank the king liked so much.

He saw the orc tying ropes to the airplane and pounding stakes into the ground. He wondered if it was the famous orc pilot that the prince had made a knight.

What he wanted to do was kill the orc and order the woman off their island. He couldn't, of course. It was her island and they were tenants. They weren't serfs, but they might as well be. None of them had any place to go on the main island.

All that was going through his mind as he, his wife, and his brother in law approached them.

Betty Cartwright waved. "Hello!" she shouted. "I hope we didn't mess up anything. This looked like the best place to land."

"We're going to need a hangar if the winds are like this very often," said the orc.

Michael looked at the orc, then at the woman. He spoke to the woman. "The winds are usually like this. There's not much to stop them or slow them on the island."

The woman looked back at him and her expression went from friendly, even apologetic, to firm, even hard. "I am Countess Green Isle and this is *my* pilot, Paul Fortonson. His brother is Sir Yahg Fortonson. You will need to discuss the hangar and the needs of the aircraft with him."

* * *

Paul noticed the islander's gaze pass over him, refusing to acknowledge his existence. He didn't like it, but he was used to it. Then, Pip, now Betty Cartwright, called the man on it. He wasn't sure what to do, and wished he was back in Parise, where all he had to deal with was Pariseians trying to kill him. Over the last months, he'd learned to be an airplane mechanic and a pilot. He'd flown scouting missions and been Yahg's pilot on bombing runs. And, for perhaps the first time in his life, he'd been accepted by most of the men around him. He was a soldier among soldiers and a skilled specialist who was providing valuable intelligence to the officers in command of the army. He'd been of use and everyone knew it. Most of them acknowledged it, following the prince's example. He'd also been involved in killing people and that part he didn't like. Didn't like it at all.

So Yahg had arranged this. When a plane got assigned to Betty, Paul was assigned as her pilot. Paul felt more than a little guilty about that, but he really didn't want to drop bombs on people, not if he had any other choice.

* * *

Michael looked at her and realized that she could throw him out of his home. He bowed. He didn't want to, but he did. Then, steeling himself, he looked at the orc and was surprised that the orc didn't look any happier with her orders than he was. "Sir Paul, what is a hangar?"

"I'm no sir. The prince knighted my brother, not me, and it's a life title, non-inherited." Paul shrugged. "I'm told I count as an esquire now, but my father was a bone picker until he got the job at the airplane factory. And he's a good enough man for all that.

"A hanger is a building, wood or stone, that you put an airplane in to keep it out of the wind and the weather. There is usually a large door in the front and it's attached at the top so it can be lifted up to let the plane in and out. You put the hangar next to the landing field."

Michael looked at the countess, then back at the orc. No, at Paul. "Seems like a lot of work."

"It is, but it can be worth it. With the airplane here, a sick child can be gotten to a healer in Londinium in two hours. Medicines and tools can be brought to the island as needed. If you'll come with me, I'll show you some of the stuff we brought this trip." He waved at Michael just like a person, and turned back to the airplane.

Not having any other option, and not having any experiences with orcs, Michael followed him, and so did his brother in law. His wife stayed to see to the countess's needs. The Isle of Green didn't have a residence suitable for a countess. No king or prince had ever visited here. Only the king's rent collector, and he only came once a year and stayed in the island's one and only inn.

* * *

At the airplane, Paul took out several magical items. There were potions and devices. He also brought out surveying equipment. The last time the island had been surveyed was for the tax book back in 753.

"Is there clay or sand on the island?" Paul was asking as he pulled another box out of the storage area behind the passenger compartment of the airplane.

"Yes. Why?"

Paul pointed at the box. "That's a magical microwave kiln."

"A what?" John Finch, Michael's brother in law, asked.

"I'm not sure either. It's made by Freedric the wizard and Alvin the bard based on some weird old dwarven books."

That wasn't the truth, but it was a standard cover story and what all but a select few believed. Paul repeated it with the ease of long practice. In fact, microwaves were magically produced in the container and vitrified the clay. But it worked if you crafted the spell into it, and Paul, after the last two weeks of practice, knew the spell well enough to load the item. He wasn't a wizard like his sister, but he could load a variety of magical items.

"I'll show you how to load the spell into it and we'll be able to make ceramics without the need of forests." He looked around. "Which seem to be in short supply."

Location: Isle of Green, Kingdom Isles
Time: Mid Morning, 9 Barra, 990AF

Paul pointed the nose into the wind and brought the plane down onto the airfield. The hangar hadn't been started yet, but the stakes and the windsock were up, which helped. He'd spent the night in Londinium and Countess Green Isle was still there, working at the bank and going all dewy eyed over Albert. That was okay with Paul. He liked Albert Royce. He yawed the plane a bit to the left to compensate for the wind and decreased the power. And the plane touched down. He taxied to the tie downs and climbed out.

John Finch was there waiting, and helped him with the tie downs and the unloading. In order to set up a cannery and some other businesses on the Isle of Green, they were going to need a lot of gear. Some of it would be magical and engineering, or just mechanical. John was very interested in the airplane and other gadgets.

"What did you bring us this time, lad?" John asked.

"Cold boxes," Paul said. "Shrunk cold boxes." The shrink spell let Paul bring a great deal more cargo per trip than he'd have been able to without it.

They carried the stuff, still shrunk, to the ox drawn cart that John Finch had brought and went to the village about half a mile away. They unloaded and stored the stuff, then everyone went back to work. New countess or not, they had sheep to shear, goats to milk, and crops to get in.

Paul took off his shirt and joined them in the field as they brought in the oats. He would spend the night here and fly back to Londinium in the morning.

Location: Gwinevere Palace, Londinium
Time: Mid Morning, 10 Barra, 990AF

King Arthur III looked at the representative of the House of Lords. Duke Dandridge was his second cousin and not a friend. "You've given these gadgets to your favorites. And the lords of the realm will *not* stand for it."

"I'm not giving them to anyone," Arthur said. He was fully aware that his cousin Ronald thought that he should be the king, not Arthur. But Arthur was the king and it was time to remind Ronald of that. "They belong to Albert Royce and his compatriots in the company that they founded. They applied for patents for inventions that they developed."

"Those patents should have been given to your nobles. It's our right as nobles of the Isles."

The strange thing was that Arthur, a year ago before all this started, might have agreed with Dandridge. Yes, a servant should receive a reward when he brings his lord a new device, but the device belongs to the lord, as does the servant that created it. But over months of discussions with Betty about money, property, and the rights of his subjects, Arthur had slowly come to realize that that way led to revolution.

"Those patents are the property of the people who made the products. They are patented and will remain so until the patent expires, which will be in seven years if it's not renewed, or twenty-one if they take advantage of their option to renew it twice." That too had been a suggestion from Betty Cartwright. "That is so that the inventor is encouraged to invent more, but at the end of the day, all such products become the wealth of the Kingdom as a whole. Be patient, my lord. In twenty years or so, you will be able to make your own airplane without needing a license from Royce Enterprises."

"The House of Lords has not ratified that decree."

"I am still the king, am I not?" Arthur demanded. "As king, I can grant any title or patent I see fit."

"Not for some limited duration. Not for an *idea* or *design*."

"That's an interesting statement. But I would urge you not to take it to the Crown Court. It might decide that such a grant must be permanent."

"As it should be and it should be granted to your nobles, not a knight and a bunch of peasants."

"Yahg is a knight, too," Arthur said.

"Edward must have been suffering brain fever," Duke Dandridge said.

"It doesn't seem to have affected his ability to wage war, Your Grace. Something you should remember."

"Are you threatening me?" Dandridge was pale with rage.

"No," Arthur said in a blatant lie. "Merely reminding you."

That effectively ended the meeting, and as much immediate gratification as it had given him, Arthur knew that it had been a mistake. Dandridge wasn't the only noble in the Kingdom Isles that felt that his nobility of blood entitled him to the work of others. The belief was the next best thing to universal.

The Commons was offering Arthur a great deal more support, though even there it was hardly universal. The new plows had been granted a patent just like the rest, then Royce Enterprises had given the design into the public domain, to be used by any smith in the Kingdom. That act of generosity had greatly endeared them to the small landholders, who mostly weren't going to be able to build their own plane anyway and who would just as soon buy their books, rather than print them. It gave the king a solid majority in the Commons and Edward's victories in Parise gave him a strong minority in the Lords.

* * *

As he left the palace, Ronald Alen Dandridge cursed under his breath. He hadn't expected anything else really, but Arthur had threatened him and that he would not bear. He didn't have the forces to challenge the sitting monarch, not in the Kingdom. But Parise, Nasine, even Doichry, were concerned about Freedric's airplane and what it and all the other inventions did to the balance of power.

No. As much wealth as they might provide if they were captured, it wasn't worth the risk. Freedric, Alvin, Betty, and most especially Yagh, had to die. It would take careful planning, and Ronald's hands must be kept clean. But it had to be done.

Location: Isle of Green, Kingdom Isles
Time: Mid Morning, 14 Coganie, 990AF

Paul was flying Freedric's airplane. Freedric himself was flying the new two engine, eight passenger version. Paul watched as Freedric landed the larger plane at the landing field on Green Isle and taxied it over next to the hangar. The hangar was made for this one, and the new Arthur class passenger plane's wings were too big. So it was tied down on the leeward side of the hangar.

Once it was down, Paul landed. Then he turned around and touched the amulet that Prince Edward was wearing. It was a small silver cloud on a silver chain. As Paul touched the silver cloud, Edward woke up, looked around, and smiled at Paul. "Excellent flight, Paul. You do your brother proud." He took off the amulet of sleep and gave it back to Paul. It was a gift to Paul from an intercessor of Prima. Unlike a wizard's sleep spell, it had to be invoked by the person wearing it, though it could be deactivated by anyone. It put the wearer into a deep and restful sleep for eight hours or until deactivated, whichever came first. It was a very minor spell in a magical item aged by Prima in one of her temples until it was self recharging. It could be used once a week.

Paul had received it after an intercessor he was taking to Green Isle noticed how tired he was. Prima, like Cashi, seemed fond of *the four*, as Paul thought of his brother, Betty, Freedric, and Alvin. Part of that was because Paul, Yahg, Freedric, even Alvin and Betty, though they didn't fly nearly so often, were always willing to take an intercessor of Prima anywhere their planes could reach.

They had saved a lot of lives by getting healers to those in need and those in need to a healer.

The other gods hadn't given any solid indication of how they felt about the changes *the four* were introducing.

The prince climbed out of the plane while Paul tucked the amulet into his tunic. Once the prince was with the others, Paul taxied the Skiff into the hangar and climbed out.

By the time he got to the group, the prince was talking to Intercessor Michael J. Lowrey about the necessity of Cashi introducing its own temple money.

"It's because Kingdom paper isn't accepted in Parise or really anywhere in Centraium. But Cashi's money, like Cashi's church, is present everywhere."

"Is that a good thing?" Prince Edward asked. "Sir Yahg has been lecturing me on logistics again."

"Amateurs study tactics," Freedric said. "Professionals study logistics."

"So I keep hearing," Edward said. "And I agree. But it's not just our logistics that have mattered in getting us to within a hundred miles of Ifle. The dauphin's lack of logistics has proven very helpful."

"We can't take sides, Your Highness," said Michael. "At least, the church of Cashi as a whole can't take sides. Noron isn't pleased at the degree to which money is playing a role in the contests between princes, as it is. I am a Kingdomer, but I'm also an intercessor of Cashi."

"I know, but with the Nasines coming in on the side of the Pariseians, things have gotten difficult. And the new airplanes that the Nasine and Pariseians are building aren't helping, either." He looked over at Freedric.

"We have sent the emperor of Nasine a very stern letter reminding him that we have a patent on airplanes in general, and the skiff design in particular. We even sent it by an intercessor of Justain. Not that we expect it to do any good. Nasine is another country, after all, and there is no treaty between Nasine and the Kingdom to make the patents of inventions in one enforceable in the other."

Paul was bored by the discussion. He'd heard it all before. He left them to their talk and went over to have a look at the Arthur class airplane. He found the actual Arthur already there talking with Betty Cartwright.

"Here he is, Your Majesty. This is Yahg's younger brother, Paul, who flew your son here today."

Paul tried to bow and probably made a hash of it, judging by the way the king was trying not to laugh. "I hope he flies better than he bows," King Arthur said.

"Not many orcs or half orcs have an opportunity to be presented to a king, Your Majesty. Not a lot of practice. But, Paul here has been flying back and forth and here and there everyday that wasn't too cloudy for months now."

"It was a pleasant flight, Your Majesty." Paul managed to say, "His Highness seemed pleased."

"And now he's trying to talk the church of Cashi out of making their own money. It won't work," said the king.

Paul felt himself nod and he couldn't help the grin.

"So what do you think of the Arthur?" the king asked. waving at the plane.

"It's impressive, Your Majesty, but I think I prefer the Skiff. The Arthur is faster, but less maneuverable. It could be used as a bomber, but a skiff with a wizard aboard would find it an easy target."

"A warrior's judgment," King Arthur III said. "But war isn't all there is, lad. This airplane will take me and several members of court to Eirie in a day, or take a ton of machine parts from Londinium to Normanland in an hour."

"Yes, Your Majesty," Paul said. "But the Skiff is still more fun to fly."

The king laughed.

They went to the newly built estate of Countess Green Isle, and for the next several days they discussed the Kingdom Bank, how it was doing, the oversight committee that included four members of the Commons and four members of the Lords. But the House of Lords included the lords of the temples, so included the representative of Cashi.

* * *

After the first day, Paul was released to fly errands and Freedric's Skiff spent day after day shipping supplies and people back and forth from the island to Londinium, and occasionally to Normanland, which was about at the edge of the Skiff's range from Green Isle.

CHAPTER 15: ATTACK ON THE KING

Location: Cape Louis, Parise
Time: Mid Morning, 22 Coganie, 990AF

Cape Louis was nominally under the control of the Kingdom forces at this time, but the people were Pariseians and loyal to King Louis IV, so when the wizards arrived with letters from the king, they hid them. It wasn't hard. The Kingdomers had come through a month ago, taken half the catch as taxes, and left.

Gaston de Long examined the magical wings. They were, in his opinion, crap. The magical item held the modified wing spell that the king's agent had bought from that wizard in Callbridge. Then Bernard de Colt had converted the spell into a magical item spell and built a magical item to hold it. That much was good, but this thing should have been set in a spell safe for a year at least. Better yet, a decade. He understood the necessities of war, but the hi command didn't seem to understand the necessities of magic. The damn wings were kludgy as hell, even if they were fast.

He sighed, stretched his back, and pulled out the Royceograph printed instructions, and started loading the wings. Gaston de Long was a knight of Parise and an amulet wizard. At least, his rod of lightning was good. He'd made it himself ten years ago and it had set in a spell safe until the war with the Kingdom had started.

He wasn't the only mage. There were twelve wizards in the strike force, all men of wealth and consequence, and all aware of the desperate straits of Parise.

* * *

Three hours later they put on their goggles and the backpack-sized amulets of aircraft wings, invoked them, and started flying. The amulets produced a top speed of one hundred and twenty miles per hour, which wasn't comfortable, and they flew for two to three hours, depending on the skill of the spell crafter. In this case, after two hours, they landed in the Kingdom in a forest just east of the Isle of Green. Then they started the process over again. They loaded the spell into the amulets of aircraft wings, then took off to attack Green Isle and kill Arthur, Edward, and his counselors.

Location: In the Air, Approaching Green Isle
Time: Mid Afternoon, 22 Coganie, 990AF

Paul had a load of pastries. He was flying a load of frigging pastries from the king's chef in Londinium to the conference on Green Isle. It was silly, and wasteful of the still very limited resource that airplanes were. But the king wanted the scones his chef made, and what the king wanted, the king got.

They are attacking. Flying wizards. The thought appeared in his mind. He knew it was from Alvin the Bard. He thought back *I'm coming.* He looked around the sky, looked at his batteries, pushed the power to 100 percent, and tipped the nose down. He was still two minutes out.

Location: Green Isle Estate

Prince Edward wasn't good with the pistol he'd been presented with. It was a black powder ball and cap revolver with six shots, and not magical at all. Even though it seemed like magic. He had appreciated the gift from Betty and Alvin, who'd developed the pistols. That didn't stop him from running out into Betty's courtyard, taking the pistol in both hands, pointing it at the flying wizards, and shooting. He missed. Six times. They moved so fast.

A *fireball* hit three feet from him, and he was thrown across the courtyard.

Freedric was a bit more successful with *wizard shot.* He knew to lead his target, but the attacking wizards were in wizard armor and his bolt's damage was limited. He did little more than disrupt their aim.

Betty ran out, grabbed the prince under each arm, and pulled him inside. Then she checked him, using first aid training that she'd received back in the Merge world.

Fireballs were hitting the walls of her home and there was a lot of wood in its construction, so it was going to start burning soon.

* * *

The locals came out with slings, the same slings they used to hunt the rabbits that lived on the island. They tried but had less success than the prince. All they managed to do was get the attacking wizards to waste a couple of fireballs and get three of their own killed.

* * *

Paul could see them now. They were fast, but they were also below him. He saw them finish a pass and swing around and get into something approaching a line to attack the estate again. He pulled the nose up and got some altitude.

He thought about the revolver that Betty had given him, but he didn't like his chances. Then he thought about what would happen if his very real wings were to contact the immaterial wings of the flying wizards. Not knowing what else to do, he gave it a try. Having gained a couple of thousand feet, he put the Skiff into a dive, heading almost straight down. And as he went down, his airspeed went up. He was flying at just over two hundred miles per hour as he started to pull up. He came in behind the formation, trying to hit them, to ram them with the fuselage or wings of his aircraft and hoping that he wouldn't destroy his airplane at the same time.

But Paul was a half orc, and his tribe was under attack. Even if he'd known for sure that it would destroy the Skiff and him with it, he would have done the same thing. One thing he'd totally forgotten about was the *vambraces of armor* that Betty Cartwright had given to him.

The Skiff came up and was still doing 180 as it hit the first of the wizards. The wizard was doing about one sixty and never saw the Skiff until it hit him. It knocked him for a loop and he lost control of the wings. He plowed into the ground at a hundred and sixty miles per hour.

The next one the Skiff missed. But the Skiff was traveling at 180 and at that speed, the disruption of airflow is significant. The magical wings of the wizard acted just like real wings, when hit by a massive downdraft, they went down. The wizard flying them was not experienced. He had less than ten hours of flight time. He over controlled, went into a spin and augered in. He didn't hit as hard, maybe sixty miles an hour, but that was plenty hard enough.

The Skiff took out five of the attacking wizards in that first pass. He only actually hit the first one, but the rest were too close to the disrupted airflow, too low and too inexperienced to handle the situation right. Then he was past them. The ones he hadn't taken down, he had still disrupted their flights, just not as much. Their aim was thrown off and they were terrified by the buffeting. By the time they found the Skiff in the sky, it was climbing. Three of them started climbing after the Skiff, two returned to their attack on the estate, and one, the smart one, flew east, away from the island.

Paul was in a climb. The Skiff had a cruising speed around eighty-five miles per hour. In a climb, that dropped to sixty. In a steep climb, to fifty. The flying wings were faster and more maneuverable.

It took them a while, but they were catching him by the time he hit two thousand feet.

* * *

Gaston de Long managed to keep from flying into the wall of Countess Green Isle's estate. Barely. Then he saw the Skiff, looked around and saw the bodies. Half the team of wizards. And in that moment, he knew that that airplane had to be destroyed if Parise was going to have any chance of winning this war. An attack on King Arthur that was not successful would destroy Parise. He adjusted his weight and used the magical controls to adjust his wings and flew after the Skiff, followed by two of his companions. It took a while. He was still getting used to the wings, and they were kludgy and awkward to use.

He'd never tried to climb and he almost pointed his wings too high and stalled. In fact, he did stall a little, but he managed to recover. Then he flew up at a less sharp angle. His wings were propelled forward by magic. It wasn't enough to lift him straight up, but at forty-five degrees, he could fly up. It took a while, but he was gaining. It wasn't that the wings were more powerful, but they were much much lighter.

* * *

Hubert Dumont sighted on the roof of the main building and fired a lightning bolt. The lightning bolt turned and hit a metal rod sticking up out of the roof, then followed that rod into the ground. His goggles were goggles of *see magic* and he hadn't seen any on the rod. This place had hidden protections.

He pulled up and came around again, looking around as he did. He was getting low on ammunition and as he looked around the situation was getting desperate. Half of the team were down, three were chasing that airplane. And Bruno had run for home.

The courtyard was empty. They had retreated inside.

* * *

Yahg was at the arms locker. Guns are simple things. The mass production of guns isn't simple. One rifle takes three to four pounds of steel. A thousand rifles take three or four thousand pounds. The Kingdom army wouldn't have rifles for years. But Betty's house had three handmade rifles, with scopes. One difference between a rifle and a bow and arrow is a bullet travels a lot faster than an arrow. You still have to lead a moving target, but not by nearly as much.

He got the locker opened and pulled out a scoped rifle. It was a breech loading cap lock with paper cartridges. It opened like an old fashioned shotgun and the paper cartridge was cut when it was closed. That left loose powder in the path of the flame when the cap was hammered. It was what they'd been able to come up with. Yahg grabbed a handful of cartridges and ran up the stairs to the third floor. Betty's new house was three stories tall.

Once he got upstairs he went to a window and opened it, then laid the barrel on the window sill and looked for a target.

* * *

Hubert Dumont noticed the window opening and headed for it. Maybe he could put a fireball in the room. That should start the building on fire.

Something stuck out the window. He targeted the window. Just a little closer. . . .

There was a bang like thunder, but sharper, and he felt agony in his left foot. It distracted him and for two vital seconds, he wasn't in control of the wings. He rammed into the building seven feet from the window Yahg was shooting from.

The walls were wooden boards imported from the main island by ship. And Hubert went through the wall he hit about half way. He was traveling at over a hundred miles per hour, after all.

The shock almost knocked Yahg out of the window.

* * *

In the air, the three wings were gaining on the Skiff, but their relative velocity wasn't all that great. With no better idea, Paul pulled out his pistol. He looked over to the left. There was a man flying. One hand was on a stick, the other was holding what Paul guessed was a rod of something. Maybe fireball, maybe lightning bolt. Maybe even wizard bolt.

The Skiff had an enclosed cockpit but the windows in the doors could be opened by unlatching a latch then pulling the window down into the door frame. Paul thought it was a great design, even if Betty complained about the lack of a crank.

He opened the window and stuck the pistol out. The wind almost took it out of his hand. But he braced his arm against the back of the door frame and pointed it at the goggled flier forty feet to his left and gaining on him.

While he was doing that, the flier was pointing his rod at Paul. Paul shot and missed. The flier shot and missed, possibly startled by the noise the pistol made.

Paul shot again. He hit. He wasn't sure where, but the fellow spun away and was lost to sight. Then there was a fireball next to him. It singed his left wing and Paul put the stick hard over and banked hard right. Then he flipped into an upside down dive.

He looked back over his shoulder, looking for the other flyers.

* * *

Gaston de Long felt the bullet slam into his right leg and, like Hubert, lost control of the wings for a few moments. In Gaston's case, it didn't kill him. He had plenty of air room, but he was in a spin. By the time he started trying to control the wings, he'd also dropped his rod of fireballs. And there was something else. The wings weren't designed for this sort of stress. They were controlled by a stick, but the spell that they were based on was designed to let a book wizard fly as fast as a plane. Not swoop and turn and maneuver. Every time they made a sharp turn, it stressed the magic of the wings. And the wings were starting to lose their lift, their shape was starting to distort. The smooth laminar flow of air that Thomas McKendrick had envisioned was becoming rough. And the parasitic drag that Thomas McKendrick's spell almost eliminated was back with a vengeance. Right now it was pulling his left wing back while his right wing tried to leap ahead. So, with a hole in his right leg, Gaston tried to control an amulet of flying that was losing its spell.

He managed it because he was very good. He got down to the ground in one piece, but then the spell died. It would take him an hour to recraft the thing if the degrading spell hadn't ruined the amulet.

* * *

Paul was having his own troubles. He'd briefly escaped the two flying wizards that were chasing him by his dive, but they'd dived too and coordinated while they did. They'd separated and were coming at him from two directions. To escape one, he'd have to face the other. He kept going down until he was only a couple of hundred feet up, then he pulled out straight at one of them. Maybe he could repeat that first maneuver.

* * *

Back on the ground, His Highness Prince Edward had recovered consciousness and reloaded his pistol. The prince was a natural leader and amazingly brave. As soon as his pistol was loaded again, he went back out into the courtyard, over Betty's strong objections.

Arthur wasn't a coward by any means, but he wasn't crazy. He agreed with Betty, but he knew his son and knew that nothing short of main force would keep him inside.

"Leave it, Countess. My son is an idiot." He looked up, trying to make sense out of the chaos of battle. A battle in three dimensions, but Arthur was familiar with battle and he had a mind that could cope with the changes a third dimension caused. He looked up at the sky. There was a wizard coming back around to target the prince, and that would bring him into the sights of both the prince and Yahg. In another part of the sky, Paul was flying the Skiff straight at the ground, followed by two flying wizards. A third flying wizard was flying in a circle, slowly coming to the ground. Arthur wasn't sure if it was a problem with the flying spell or the wizard.

Freedric and Alvin were at the arms closet loading guns, and the intercessor of Cashi, Michael J. Lowrey, was standing up from his prayers. Then Michael was running out of the building to go to the prince.

Freedric and Alvin ran out into the courtyard but to different places. Arthur realized that the flying wizard couldn't target them all at once but they could all target him.

Michael reached the prince, laid a hand on him and said, "Lead," invoking the spell that Cashi had just given him.

Then the flying wizard was there and everyone was shooting. Freedric and Yahg each shot a rifle. Alvin and the prince each shot their pistols dry, and the wizard landed in a heap in the courtyard.

The moment he did, Arthur was pointing at the sky. "Look at Paul!" he shouted.

For Paul was just pulling out of his dive straight at one of the flying wizards.

* * *

Paul pulled up, pointed at one of the wizards, and the wizard fired a fireball. It went past him, but the wizard fired another, and that one hit the plane. The Skiff was covered in canvas and doping. The doping was mostly tree resin. Dried tree resin.

In a moment, the Skiff was engulfed in flame and burning. Paul kept it pointed right at the wizard. They hit a second later and the Skiff shattered the wizard, but that was one shock too many. The wings came off and the Skiff plowed into the ground.

* * *

Yahg saw it from the window and then was running down the stairs.

Prince Edward saw Paul take out the wizard, but didn't see the crash. He could guess well enough the plane had been on fire.

He ran for the gate, reloading his pistol as he went.

Freedric, Alvin, and Betty were all right after him. Arthur followed, but more slowly.

* * *

Benoît de Blanc looked around. The sky was empty. Twelve. There had been twelve powerful amulet wizards in the strike force, provided with powerful magics, and he was all that was left. This was a disaster and the king must be informed. He turned his wings to the east and flew away.

* * *

The prince was walking. It was some distance to where the Skiff was burning in a plowed field. The others caught up to him. First, Freedric and Alvin, then Betty.

"I would have knighted him had he lived," Prince Edward said. "For he did the lion's share of the fighting, and even in the end, his courage didn't falter.

"I'm going to knight him anyway," Betty said. "Let his parents and sister gain the granted lands."

By that time Yahg and the king caught them. Prince Edward looked at the king, then at Yahg and asked, "Will you allow that, Father? Allow an orcish family to be landed knights? For as long as their line should last?"

Arthur looked at Yahg, who's face looked to be made of stone. He thought about the ramifications. It would cost him. Perhaps a hundred votes in the Commons and a dozen in the Lords. And yet, if ever one of his had done more, he could not recall it. On his back was Excalibur, the sword of the original Arthur Pendragon with his Knights of the Table Round. And he reached up and took that hilt in his hand. Excalibur had no doubts. He could feel it. "Nay. I'll do the knighting. By Excalibur. Let them argue with that."

There were limits on how many knights could sit at the round table in castle Guiniver. The king and eighteen knights. At the moment though, there were only ten, for Excalibur would not rest on the shoulder of any unworthy.

* * *

They continued to walk, and as they got closer they could see the plane. The wings had ripped loose some twenty feet above the ground. The fuselage had landed and bounced, then flipped, absorbing the force a little at a time, and finally the pilot's chair had flown through the shattered window to land thirty feet farther on. And, still strapped into it, was the body of Paul Fortonson.

The body moved.

Groaned. Looked around bleary eyed. One hand started scrambling around for something. Then he screamed as the hand demonstrated that it was broken.

"He's alive!" Betty shouted.

It took a while to figure out how. Part of it was simply that the Skiff was a heck of a lot better designed than anything that had flown before 1930 in the world that Jerry Garman had lived in. Part of it was that the Skiff was a slow aircraft. It hadn't crashed into the ground at half the speed of sound. It had crashed at no more than forty miles per hour. But the final piece of the puzzle were the vambraces of armor that they had found in the dwarven magic safe. One had gone to Alvin, and the other to Pip. When Yahg had become the pilot for the prince, Alvin had given him his pair. When Betty was made Countess Green Isle, she'd been pretty sure she wouldn't be in any more knife fights and had given her pair to Paul, who was going to be going to war with his brother. Magic armor absorbs damage and this was powerful armor. The shattering force of the crash was mostly taken up by the armor. It would take the armor a few days to restore itself but it had done its job.

They got Paul out of the still burning plane and he had a broken hand, two broken legs, and his green beard was burned off. His hair had been under his leather flying helmet and his eyes behind goggles, so they were fine. Paul looked less orcish than his older brother. He was a big young man, but the green fur that covered Yahg's body was more of a green down in the case of Paul and Elizabeth.

By that time the locals had arrived. Their village was near, but not next to the new countess' estate. More to the point, when wizards are attacking from the sky, a smart person stays out of sight, and out of the fight.

John Finch, the mayor's brother in law, had become friends with Paul over the months since the Skiff had first landed. He even helped the lad with the plane. To a lesser extent, so had the rest of the villagers. They actually had more contact with Paul and the rest of Betty's staff than they had with Betty. She was the countess and, besides, she spent most of her time in Londinium. Paul was here a couple of days a week and he usually brought something useful to the island as well as to the countess' estate.

John and his wife rushed to Paul's aid, then he and several other villagers ran and fetched a stretcher to take Paul back to the estate.

The jokes they told about hard headed orcs weren't particularly sensitive, but the truth was the jokes they told about each other weren't much different, and there was real concern for a friend under the rough humor. They discussed the thickness of orcish sculls and the little room left for brains. But even as they did they were handling the young half orc with care and concern. And several of the young ladies of the village were sighing at how heroic he'd been.

* * *

Prince Edward watched the villagers take Paul back to the estate, then looked around. "Where did that wizard go down? The one that was going around in circles as he came down," he asked.

Yahg, who'd been on the third floor, pointed. The prince started off, with Yahg and two of the older villagers.

King Arthur shouted after them. "We want him alive."

The prince waved acknowledgement.

"How's it going to feel to have to defer to your little brother, Yahg?"

"What?" Yagh asked, then added, "Oh, yes. Table Round."

"What's that, Sir Yahg?" Michael Jones, the mayor of the island, asked. By now he was fairly comfortable around folk with green hair, though Sir

Yahg did look more orcish than his younger brother. But he was *a lot* more comfortable around orcs than princes.

"After the battle, His Majesty said he was going to knight my idiot brother with Excalibur."

"Can he do that with an orc?" Jones asked, then quickly added, "No offense. I'm fond of the boy, I am. But . . ."

It was Prince Edward who answered. "It will be up to Excalibur. The sword has a mind of its own. If Excalibur hadn't liked the idea, my father would have known." The prince stopped speaking, but not walking, as he considered. "It is a bit surprising, considering the way elves feel about orcs."

"What does that have to do with it?" Yahg asked.

"What? Is there actually something you don't know?" Prince Edward asked with a grin.

"Yes, Your Highness," Yahg admitted. "Two, perhaps three, things."

"So many? Then let us reduce the number. Excalibur is an elven blade. Forged by the wood of an elven tree in the Elven Lands. It's said that the sword holds the soul of an elven mage. And having held it, I can attest that someone lives in that blade. It has a will of its own and perceives the world in a way that's strange, but insightful."

Jones and the other two villagers who had followed were watching this exchange with gobsmacked expressions. Then Yahg held up a hand and the prince froze between one step and the next. It took the villagers a moment more, and one of them nearly stepped on the prince's heels.

Yahg made some gestures that meant nothing to the villagers, but the prince nodded.

Yagh slipped away through the scrub, and the prince turned to the villagers. "Yahg heard something," he whispered. "Just over that rise. You wait here. We don't want him alerted.: Then the prince moved away much slower than Yahg and not quite as quietly.

* * *

Yahg moved through the scrub. It was winter and the bushes that the locals used as fire wood were mostly leafless and dry. It made it hard to sneak up on people, but it also made it hard to hide. As soon as his head topped the small rise, he saw the wizard with his head in a book, his backpack off and trying to craft a spell into it.

He thought about a sling stone, but no. It would probably kill the bastard and the king wanted him alive. For that matter, Yahg wanted him alive.

Moving as quietly as he could, Yahg drifted left to put him behind the wizard.

Then he moved closer. *Just keep concentrating on your spell crafting, fellow,* he thought. It took him five minutes, and he could see the prince ten yards back.

When he was ten feet from the wizard, there was a sound from the rise. The wizard's head popped up. He looked at the rise and fired a wizard bolt from a rod. Yahg lept two running steps and he was on the wizard. He slammed his gauntleted hand against the wizard's hand, the one holding the rod. With the other arm going around the wizard's chest, he took them both to the ground. The magic of the spell that the wizard was trying to craft into the flying pack was already distorted. The wizard had been trying to craft the spell in pain from the bullet wound in his right leg. He was also losing blood, so he was a bit woozy. Being thrown onto the half completed spell, half installed into the amulet of flying was just the final straw.

The spell didn't dissipate. It exploded.

That, at least, was how it seemed to Yahg who, along with the wizard, was thrown thirty feet into the air and then fell back onto the ground. With the damned idiot wizard on top of him.

Yahg, too, was wearing the centuries old dwarven vambraces of armor. He didn't even break anything. He did have the wind knocked out of him.

The wizard was unconscious.

* * *

By the time they got back to the estate of Countess Green Isle, Paul was already installed in a bed and looking quite pleased with himself.

Michael J. Lowrey, High Intercessor of Cashi for the Kingdom Isles, was all out of magic for the day. He'd used *lead* to help the prince lead his shot at the wizard. And the one healing spell he had, had been used on Paul.

Yagh and the wizard were bandaged up and put in beds next to Paul.

After the amulet wizard had been stripped naked and every amulet he owned taken from him.

CHAPTER 16: SIR PAUL

Location: Green Isle Estate
Time: Near Dawn, 23 Coganie, 990AF

Paul woke to a very painful hand and looked around. His big brother was two beds away and a man was in the cot between them. He tried to sit up and fell back in the bed. His hand wasn't the only thing broken. He tried to piece together what had happened. It was all very disjointed. Bits and pieces, fireballs, and that was it. Wizards attacking the countess' estate.

He looked at the man in the center cot. "Didn't I shoot you?"

It was hard to tell. The fellow had been wearing goggles and a flight helmet.

"*Oui*, I think so." After a moment's consideration, the man continued, "I hold no grudge. I was trying to shoot you with a fireball at the time."

"Worse than that. You were trying to kill my king."

"War." The fellow shrugged in a very Pariseian manner.

"Doesn't normally include the attempted assassination of a head of state," came Yahg's voice from the other side of the Pariseian wizard.

"I had my orders. I obeyed them. Or tried to."

"What's your name?" Yahg asked.

"Cavalier Gaston de Long. And you?"

"That's Sir Yahg Fortonson," Paul said.

That was when Betty came in, followed by Michael Lowery. "Michael is going to heal Paul a little more. And you will be happy to know that Freedric has taken the Arthur-class plane back to Londinium and will be bringing an intercessor of Prima who gets more magic than Michael does."

"I have other talents, Countess," Michael said.

"I know, Michael," Betty agreed. "What did Louis think he was doing?" she asked, turning to Gaston de Long.

"I don't know, Countess Green Isle," Gaston said, but it lacked the ring of truth to Paul's ear.

"What do you suspect, Gaston?" he asked.

Gaston looked at him and almost sniffed. Paul could tell the Pariseian knight felt that being questioned by an orc was beneath him. Paul felt his face go red. Orcs tended to have pale skin under their fur. Blushes and anger showed.

"It's a fair question," said Betty Cartright.

"And an astute one," said Michael with a nod to Paul. "What do you suspect? Was it just King Arthur, or was the King of Parise also targeting the church of Cashi?"

Gaston de Long looked at the intercessor of Cashi for a thoughtful moment. "I don't think so, though I suspect that Countess Green Isle, Freedric the Wizard, Alvin the Bard, and even Yahg the Orc *were* targets."

"See Yahg," said Prince Edward. "Now, don't you wish I hadn't knighted you? You wouldn't have been a target of Louis' treachery."

Paul was shocked by how the prince's voice went from amused to enraged in the course of that single sentence.

Yahg shrugged and he didn't sound angry when he spoke. "It would have made no difference, Your Highness. It's not like I was going to go for a beer and leave you and the rest to fight it out without me."

"Which is why my son knighted you," said King Arthur, who had followed his son into the sick room. It was getting a little crowded. Then the king looked at Paul. He smiled a little, then looked at Yahg. "Well, Yahg, have you pounded on your little brother for being a reckless fool?"

"There hasn't been time, Your Majesty."

"Well, you've missed your chance then." That was when Paul noticed that King Arthur was dressed in full regalia. The king normally dressed in a doublet and hose, just like any knight might. The ermine robe and the gilded chain mail were not part of his usual dress. Paul had never seen the king in mail of any sort. And he was wearing Excalibur. The sword of state of the Kingdom Isles always traveled with the king, but he rarely wore it. After all, it was almost five feet long. But now it was sticking up over his left shoulder, ready to be drawn by his right hand.

Paul's big brother shook his head in evident disgust. "It probably wouldn't do any good, Your Majesty. The kid's head is full of rocks."

King Arthur laughed. Then he drew Excalibur with a smooth, easy grace that belied his age. As the sword came free of the scabbard, it started to sing. It wasn't vibrating or whistling through the air. It was singing in a contralto voice and, Paul thought, probably in elvish. He didn't know the words, but they had a liquidy sound to them. They flowed. The sword wasn't steel nor mithril or any other metal. It was wood. Paul could see the grain. And yet, it was so sharp that the edges were translucent, and the whole thing glowed with a golden light. Paul stared, mesmerized.

Suddenly Paul could understand the singing of the sword. It was asking him, demanding of him, that he defend the right, defend the mistreated weak against the cruel but strong, defend the Kingdom Isles against all invaders. And on and on. With every question, an event from his past was brought to mind and judged. It was humiliating and exalting at the same time, for every flaw in his character was laid bare before that song. But so was his courage, and his desire to protect his sister and family and Betty Cartwright and an ever widening circle of friends.

"Yes," Paul said. "I swear and accept the geas." For it was a geas, a compulsion that went back to the days the dwarven empire had ruled the Kingdom Isles and treated humans, orcs, and elves as chattel. The sword came down and touched him on his left shoulder, then his right.

"You can't!" It was shouted by Gaston de Long.

Paul turned to look at the man.

But it was King Arthur who laughed and spoke. "Only Excalibur can refuse to make a Knight of the Table Round. And Excalibur accepts Sir Paul Fortonson as one of her knights." He looked around the room. Bear witness, one and all.

"*Her* knights?" Betty asked.

"Yes. Excalibur is what remains of an Elven mage who fought with the First Arthur Pendragon against the Dwarven conquerors. She was too close to death when he put her into the tree, and what came out was this blade. She decides who shall be a Knight of the Table Round, and in that room we are all equal."

Gaston de Long was staring.

The story of Excalibur was told all across Centraium. Excalibur wasn't the sword in the stone. It was delivered to Arthur later. That part was known. The part that he'd just heard wasn't. At least, Paul had never heard it, and from the expression on his face, Gaston hadn't either.

"But he's an orc. Elves hate orcs," Gaston de Long insisted.

Paul was starting to find Gaston's attitude quite irritating. At the same time, it was the same attitude he'd grown up with his whole life.

"Excalibur sees deeper," Arthur said and Paul knew it was true, for the spirit of the ghost in the sword had examined him down to his core.

The king sheathed Excalibur and went to Gaston. "Enough. It's not for you to question Excalibur's judgment. Now, tell me what you think Louis had in mind with this folly."

"You're changing too much too fast. Money, magic, airplanes, and steam engines. Electric lights, and knighting orcs. It's all too much, and not just for His Majesty. The Emperor of Nasine isn't any happier, along with your own great lords." Gaston clamped his mouth shut.

King Arthur waved a casual hand. "I can make a good guess at which nobles." He turned to Paul. "And don't you go chopping heads, Paul, as tempting as that thought is. Not without evidence, which we don't have. They are nobles, after all."

That got a disgusted grunt from Yahg and Arthur looked at him.

"One set of rules for nobles and another for the common folk," Yahg said. "It's not right, Your Majesty. Not just."

Before Excalibur had chosen him, Paul had listened to his changed older brother's notions with something that was almost contempt. It wasn't that they were bad, but they weren't for the real world. Now, though, Paul knew down in the deepest corner of his soul that Excalibur agreed with Yahg.

"Excalibur agrees," Paul blurted.

"I know, Sir Paul," said King Arthur. "I wear her, after all. And she's been getting more and more restive ever since we first saw Freedric's airplane land in Londinium.

"But I can't restrict the rights of the nobles. I don't have the power."

"Then expand the rights of the commoners," Betty said.

"Frederick Douglass," Paul said.

"What do you know about Frederick Douglass?" Betty asked.

Paul laughed. "My brother likes to lecture."

"Enough, said Prince Edward. "We can discuss this at another time." He gave Gaston de Long a none to friendly look.

Location: Green Isle Estate
Time: Near Noon, 25 Coganie, 990AF

Being a Knight of the Table Round imparted certain benefits. Benefits beyond those that officially accrued. Paul healed faster than he had before, and he'd not been sickly since he'd started sleeping in the sun.

He was up and around, though still hobbling a bit and eager to get back into the air. He heard the bell and said, "Crap. I'm late."

Sally Jones, the mayor's daughter, pulled back from the embrace they'd been sharing. "Late for what?"

"Lunch with the king!" Paul said, adjusting his tunic. Sally adjusted hers and waved him away.

"Then, you'd better run, Sir Paul." She grinned.

* * *

Paul was late. Not very, but a few minutes and the king, prince, Yahg, Betty, Freedric, and Alvin were already seated. Yahg pointed at a chair. It wasn't the one Paul was expecting. The king was at the head of the table. At his right was the prince. The empty chair Yahg was pointing at was on the king's left. Feeling quite out of place, Paul went to the chair and sat.

"Now that we're all here," said the king, "what were you saying about Frederick Douglass? He was a noble bandit in that other world you're from? Do I have that right?"

"No," said Freedric, Betty, and Alvin at the same time. Yahg just grunted.

"I'm not exactly sure who he was either, Your Majesty. I just thought he was a run away orc," Paul said.

"Closer," said Alvin. "Frederick Douglass was a famous abolitionist from our world." Then, seeing the confused expressions, he added,

"Someone who was opposed to slavery. Who wanted to abolish the practice. He was an eloquent speaker and very persuasive. He was also an escaped slave."

"Okay. Now that we know who he was, what did you mean shouting about him?"

Paul tried to remember. Yahg was always quoting him, ever since the Merge. Then he had it. "When a man has a bad master, he wishes for a good master. When he has a good master he wants the best master. But when he has the best master, he wants to be his own master."

"What are you talking about, Sir Paul?" Prince Edward asked.

"A king is kind of like a master. So is a prince, even a noble like Countess Green Isle." He looked around. Paul was frightened, but he was also under a geas. And it turned out that the geas didn't just apply to fighting. "You're a good master, Your Majesty. Maybe even the best master that Frederick Douglass was talking about. Not all of your nobles are, but that's not what he was talking about. Ultimately, it's always going to be about people being their own masters."

"Each man a king in his own home," Alvin said.

"Each person," Betty corrected with a smile.

Paul nodded. "The great nobles already have that. At least, close to it. But the peasants, the villagers, the serfs . . . not so much. You can't take rights away from the great nobles, but you can give them to the peasants."

"Not that easily," Arthur said. "Every right I give to a serf on a great lord's estate is a power I take away from the great lord."

It was true. Paul knew that and he didn't have any good answers. Yahg had always been his protector. But before the Merge, never his advisor. Now, not knowing what else to do, Sir Paul looked to his big brother.

"You won't be able to do it all at once," Yahg said. He wasn't speaking to Paul. He was talking to Arthur Pendragon, King of the Kingdom Isles. "You won't live to see it. Probably your son won't either." He looked at

Prince Edward. "I won't live to see it. Paul might, if he's lucky. If not, he'll live to see it well begun."

"See what?" asked Prince Edward.

"The enfranchisement of the people of the Kingdom Isles," Yahg said. "I think that is why my little brother is a Knight of the Table Round." He looked at the others who had merged. "It couldn't be one of us. By now our special status is known, even if not generally understood. It had to be an ordinary person completely of this world. To fit the legends, it had to be about valor, this first time at least." Then Yahg stopped and looked at Paul. He looked at Paul for so long that Paul was starting to get nervous.

"I'm sorry, little brother, but also more proud than I can say," Yahg finally said, "that this burden should fall on you."

Fear and uncertainty came pouring out. Because Paul was a half orc, it came out as anger. "What in the nine hells are you talking about?"

"Paul, you get to be this world's Frederick Douglass. Its Sergeant York or Audie Murphy. Possibly it's Martin Luther King or John Adams."

"That's an awful lot to lay on one man," Alvin said. "Way too much to lay on anyone."

"Yes," Yahg agreed. "It won't all fall on Paul. And it wouldn't be possible without Betty's knowledge of money, Alvin's knowledge of electronics, and even Freedric's airplane. Those are the tools that will make the change possible by replacing enough human labor with machines to make it doable. But Paul will be the symbol, the rallying cry, the man that will let people believe that social change is possible. That's something no piece of tech can do. Not even Freedric's airplane.

CHARACTERS

Royal Society of Magic: The equivalent of the Royal Society of London

Tukerizations

Marcy Louise Caris: healer leaning antiseptic practices

Fred Wilson: Alchemist works on batteries

Michael J. Lowrey: High Intercessor of Cahsi for the Kingdom Isles.

Made up

Albert Royce: Eldest of four Royce children and the heir

Alvin the Bard: 22, fifth level bard merged with Tim Walters, 5"10' brown wavy hair and green eyes in a tanned face.

Arthur John Pendragon: King Arthur III of the Kingdom Isles, is 67 years old with long white hair.

Brian Royce: 8th level amulet wizard played by Brian Davis. Dies, doesn't merge.

Charles Royce: Sim of the original younger brother of Brian

Ronald Alen Dandridge: Cousin of the King but not an ally.

Daniel Alexander: Professor of Magical Structures, Callbridge.

Debra Royce: Sim of the original younger sister of Brian

Elizabeth: Yahg's sister named after her human grandmother

Emily Royce: Albert's daughter

Franklin Hunter: A skilled wood carver.

Forton Yahgson: Yahg's father, an orc. The last name isn't legal but Orc custom.

Freedric the Incompetent: 24, fourth level book wizard. less than a year from the mage academy in Callbridge. Merged with Jerry Garman. 5'5", black hair, black eyes, brown skin.

Glenda: Tavern Keeper

John Cloverton: Money lender. Fifties, jowly, with graying mutton chops.

John Gray: Lord John Gray Chancellor of the Exchequer.

Mack the Cudgel: Thieves Council

Maggs: Thieves Council

Paul: Yahg's younger brother is named after his human grandfather

Peter Tenhoks: Duke of the South March of Wiles and Albert's liege lord.

Pete the Cat: Thieves Council

Pip the Thief: fifth level thief, female, hides her gender. Merged with Betty Cartwright(Davis)

Thomas McKendrick: Wizard graduate of Callbridge College, teaching assistant

Tommy the Black:Thieves Council

Yahg Fortonson the Warrior: 6th level Halforc warrior, not that bright. Merged with John Kipler computer programmer, very bright

Made in the USA
Las Vegas, NV
29 June 2024

91670388R00128